D0384257

fever-hot
Dreams

ALSO BY ELLORA'S CAVE AUTHORS

All She Wants

By Jaid Black, Dominique Adair & Shiloh Walker

Taming Him

By Kimberly Dean, Summer Devon & Michelle M. Pillow

fever-hot Dreams

SHERRI L. KING
JACI BURTON
SAMANTHA WINSTON

POCKET BOOKS

NEW YORK   LONDON   TORONTO   SYDNEY

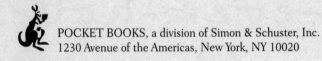 POCKET BOOKS, a division of Simon & Schuster, Inc.
1230 Avenue of the Americas, New York, NY 10020

This book is a work of fiction. Names, characters, places and incidents are products of the author's imagination or are used fictitiously. Any resemblance to actual events or locales or persons, living or dead, is entirely coincidental.

Copyright © 2007 by Ellora's Cave Publishing, Inc.
Icarus copyright © 2002 by Sherri L. King
Dream On copyright © 2005 by Jaci Burton
Darla's Valentine copyright © 2003 by Samantha Winston

Published by arrangement with Ellora's Cave Publishing, Inc.

All rights reserved, including the right to reproduce
this book or portions thereof in any form whatsoever.
For information address Pocket Books, 1230
Avenue of the Americas, New York, NY 10020

ISBN-13: 978-1-4165-3601-7
ISBN-10:   1-4165-3601-9

This Pocket Books trade paperback edition February 2007

10 9 8 7 6 5 4 3 2 1

POCKET and colophon are registered trademarks of Simon & Schuster, Inc.

Manufactured in the United States of America

For information regarding special discounts for bulk purchases,
please contact Simon & Schuster Special Sales at 1-800-456-6798
or business@simonandschuster.com

Contents

fever-hot
Dreams

Icarus

SHERRI L. KING

One

MORRIGAN MEDEROS LOOKED at the large manor house beyond the gate. After several quiet moments she inched the vehicle forward and tried to still the racing of her heart. A strange and niggling fear was prevalent in her mind and heart as she surveyed her surroundings. The house looked like a mausoleum—dark and brooding under its heavy canopy of rowan and oak trees. The atmosphere of the place sent shivers of apprehension down her spine.

But this was to be her home now, she reminded herself. This large monument of brick, stone, and mortar was to be her haven. As far away from the bustling stress of her former New York lifestyle as she could manage. She'd taken this last step of leaving her public life as a poet and songwriter behind her. Now was not the time to let her fears ruin whatever happiness she might find here.

There was no turning back now.

Her new home was nestled in Scotland, far from the incessant demands of her fans and colleagues. Far enough, too, from the dreams that had begun to rob her of her rest . . . and of her sanity. Although this land was an alien and forbidding one, it held the hope of succor during the storm her life had become.

It was cold. Morrigan tried to shake the invading chill from her bones but knew it was an effort in futility. The cool September air of Meigle, moist and chilling, could not be warded off with a mere shiver. This land, in the beautiful Valley of Strathmore, was ever damp and chilly this time of year.

The house was nestled on a plot of land on the outskirts of the village of Meigle—the oldest village in Scotland. It had existed well before the time of Christ. The ancient Picts had lived and worshipped here; their sacred standing stones even now resided in a local museum. King Arthur's stone, as well as the Macbeth stone, resided in their eternal resting places nearby. This was an ancient and mystical place, perfectly suited for her artist's temperament.

It was a magical land.

Deep in her soul she felt sure that this place could bring her the peace and happiness she sought. A peace from the days spent feeling lonely amidst an ever-growing crowd of people. From the faceless mass of people who wanted nothing from her but what her gifts and talents could bring to them.

In recent years she'd forgotten all happiness. She hoped this move would inspire it again. In the years she'd spent climbing to the top of the entertainment industry, she'd forgotten what true joy was. Her life had become an endless drive for critical acclaim. It was something she'd never wanted—not really.

She was ready to start anew.

With sudden hope welling inside of her heart she pulled into the courtyard of her new manor home. All apprehension was brushed aside and forgotten. Coming to an abrupt stop in front of the great oak door of the house, she cut the engine of her car and sighed. Several days before, her moving crew had arrived with what personal belongings she'd decided to keep when she'd moved out of her cold and sterile penthouse. She was more than eager to unpack and looked forward to surrounding herself with familiar comforts.

For weeks she'd toured the local countryside and acquainted herself with the population and culture of her newly adopted home. Now she was tired of her travels. In fact, it felt to her at times that she'd been traveling all her life—searching for this place from the very beginning.

Since the decision to move had been made, she'd felt cut adrift, and without purpose. Her busy life had never allowed her much time for relaxation. But now that she had all the time she'd ever need she found herself at a loss. What new direction would her life take now? Were her instincts correct in leading her to believe that something . . . monumental, lay in wait for her just over the horizon?

Morrigan was uncertain what the future held for her—but she was more than ready to find out.

As she stepped out of the car, the cold wind cut into her like a blade. Under her whipping black cloak, her waist-length copper hair was tamed into a fat braid along her back. Her long legs, lush figure, and exotic elfin features had made her an easily recognizable personality among showbiz's elite. But she wouldn't have much use for her assets here in her new world. She needed to blend in, not stand out, she thought with a smile.

Her charcoal gray pantsuit looked expensive and chic, and her matching Italian leather half boots barely made a sound as she walked across the cobblestones. She approached the front door with weak knees. Wind whistling about her, the scent of approaching rain heady in her nostrils, she reached for the iron handle.

Holding her breath she opened the door of her new home with slow, cautious movements. Risking a peek she looked into the dim foyer beyond and sighed in relief. She smiled and laughed a little to herself at her own foolish behavior. The interior looked the same as it had in the realtor's pictures. It was full of warm cheer and cozy welcome—all the feelings she associated with a good home.

It had been an impulsive thing—to buy this house sight unseen but for the realtor's Polaroids. But she'd been obsessed with it from the first. The realtor's description had stated that the home and land were situated in Scotland, near various lochs and waterways. A heady compulsion had taken her, driving her to stop at nothing in order to possess the property.

Shoes softly padding on the floor, she looked through each room of the house. Falling in love with it was easy. It was wonderful, complete with cathedral ceilings, high windows and spacious rooms. Her bedroom housed a lovely king-sized bed canopied by large falls of white gauze and satin. It was her favorite room. Walking to the French doors on the far side of the chamber, she opened them and stepped onto the balcony that lay beyond.

Dark green rowan branches lay close to the balustrade, giving the balcony a private and enclosed feeling. Morrigan breathed deeply of the crisp, cool air, savoring the surrounding silence. The calm of her new home began to seep into her world-weary bones. It grounded her and made her feel as though she was finally an accepted part of her surroundings.

With a serenity that had been a stranger to her in recent years, she turned back inside and made ready to unpack. Night was approaching. Hopefully she would have no dreams.

Sleep enclosed her like the darkness of a tomb, and the dream came upon her once again. The realism of it consumed her utterly, and she forgot that the dreams weren't real. Forgot to re-

member that in her new environment—supposedly free of worries—she was no longer supposed to have these dreams.

Her therapist had told her the dreams were just byproducts of
her stressful lifestyle—that they were fantasies produced by an
overworked imagination. But when the dreams conquered her
sleeping mind, all rational thought was forgotten. She knew only
the reality of what her dreaming mind showed her.

*Running through the dark forest in the night, her virginal white
nightgown flew behind her on the wind. Her hair lay unbound along
her back and shoulders, the darkness making the copper waves appear
as blood spilling over her. Her heart hammered in her breast. Her eyes
and cheeks burned from the cruel bite of the wind.*

Still she ran on, ever onward into the black heart of the forest.

*Hands outstretched in front of her to keep grasping branches from
scratching and ensnaring her, she barely noticed how far she fled. Her
feet were bare below the fall of the gown, but she didn't even feel the
ground beneath them. In the endless dark her eyes searched frantically. For something. For someone whom she dare not name lest she
doubt her very sanity.*

She searched for him.

*At last, she came upon the dark smooth mirror of a placid loch.
Her feet came to a stumbling halt at the shoreline. The water felt cold
as it lapped gently at her exposed toes, and she waited there with
bated breath. Clouds of mist puffed from her quivering mouth. The
heavy silence went on unbroken.*

*She tried to swallow the lump of fear and anticipation in her
throat, but found her mouth was far too dry. Suddenly, there before
her, a ripple broke the calm of the water's surface. It was followed by
another, and another, until the water splashed against her ankles from
the force of the waves.*

Morrigan gasped and bit her lip, fighting against the urge to flee as a dark head emerged from the heart of the loch. It was followed by the pale and heavily muscled form of a nude man. The man stepped over the water. His feet walked across its surface with barely a ripple as they passed. A small, mysterious smile played about his erotically sculpted lips. The sight sent her heart racing, though with fear or anticipation she couldn't say.

His onyx hair was dry and lay in soft waving curls down his back to his buttocks. Though he'd come from the water, he was completely dry, as if by magic. Standing at six and a half feet in height, he towered over her. His strongly muscled yet graceful body crowded her the closer he came.

His skin shone silver in the moonlight, and the only color he seemed to possess blazed from his eyes. His eyes were a deep purple, an impossibly inhuman shade. They burned her from beneath his sinfully heavy lashes, marking her with a possession that was impossible to deny.

Morrigan felt a thrill of fear race through her heart, and she turned to flee. With a shock, she discovered that her legs refused to budge. At last the man came to stand before her, and her eyes could not break away from his. His long, beautiful fingers reached for her and she tried to protest but no sound issued forth from her parted lips.

The man smiled and traced her cheeks with the tips of his cool fingers. He slowly moved his head down to her, until they were separated only by the space of their breaths. His burning eyes roved over her face with an unconcealed hunger. She was unable to meet the dark passions emanating from his gaze, and she closed her eyes in self-defense.

Like the gentle touch of a feather, she felt his thumbs caress her lowered lashes, and they flew open once more. The man closed his eyes, and leaned closer to her, his nostrils flaring as he breathed deeply *of her scent. His movements were inhuman, far too full of grace and suppressed power.*

His head moved about in a circular motion, as if he were rolling it about in the cloud of her scent. She wondered what he smelled upon her for she was wearing no perfume. Once again his dazzling eyes opened, and he caught her gaze for a long moment. The only sound that broke the silence was the haunting rhythm of her erratic heartbeats.

"It is you. At last you have come," he said, and his voice played out like an echo in the night. His accent was lyrical, like a sweet melody that was familiar to her though she could not place it. When his words faded into the darkness, he smiled, and his eyes glowed brighter than ever before. A possessive look filled his face before his features fell into a mask of wicked anticipation.

Over his bowed head she caught sight of the translucent wings that sprouted from his back. They were thin and membranous, and hung folded quietly behind him like the fins of a giant fish. Though they were a frightening testament to the man's inhumanity, they were nonetheless eerily beautiful, like an iridescent rainbow awash down his spine.

He was breathtaking.

Morrigan could not find her voice, nor could she turn from him. She stayed frozen in place, looking at the most beautiful man she'd ever seen, dreading what he might do next.

His hands strayed down her cheeks to her chin, which he tilted upwards, arching her neck until her flowing hair fell well below her buttocks. She closed her eyes to better savor his touch, and his hands strayed lower, across her shoulders and arms until he held her hands in his own. His silken hair brushed across her face as he leaned closer and pressed a cool kiss to her closed eyes.

Slowly, his lips warmed against her—borrowing her warmth. They traveled down over her cheeks and nose—as soft as the brush of a butterfly's wings. His breath was hot and fanned out over her face like a physical caress. Goose pimples broke out over her skin. His lips pressed to hers, softly and then more firmly as she gave no protest. The kiss deepened, and she felt a tiny pain. The sweet coppery taste of blood filled her mouth . . . and his.

Her eyes flew open in a panic. She began to struggle as his tongue lapped hungrily at the blood that welled from the cut in her lip. A ravenous look of hunger and rapture played across his face. His velvet tongue laved over the small wound before he drew her lip into his mouth—suckling and milking the blood from her with devouring kisses. An overwhelming fear took hold of her, and she at last found the strength to move.

Panicked and shoving against him, she twisted her head away, fighting his kiss when he followed. She felt as though she were awakening from a sorcerer's spell. She fought against the urge to cry out, but her struggles went unnoticed by her captor. His strength was overwhelmingly superior to hers. She moaned in a panic against his now burning lips.

He continued to feed on her mouth.

The man took a firmer hold on her hands as she continued to struggle, locking her arms to her side. Slowly, reluctantly, he pulled away from her lips. His erotic mouth was swollen and stained crimson from her blood. Though the sight should have sickened her, it served to arouse her instead. He seemed suddenly more beautiful and frightening than ever before, and it drew her for reasons she couldn't understand.

Handsome wasn't a powerful enough word to describe how she saw him now. He was too dangerous, too sinful to be labeled beautiful—though he was that too. The situation was more than dangerous.

Morrigan recognized this, but perversely she now wanted not to flee but to draw him closer. She wanted to lose herself within him like a moth to a flame, no matter the cost to her sanity.

Sensing her near surrender, the man raised her hands to his lips to press a fervent kiss to her palm. Watching him as closely as she was, Morrigan saw the brilliant flash of his fangs before his lips were buried in her hand. Fright overtook her once more. She almost fainted from the sight. A broken cry escaped her lips like the coo of a dove, and she renewed her struggles to escape him.

Her captor wasn't fazed by her struggles, nor did his hold on her weaken. Her temper slowly flared to life to couple with her fear. She hated feeling so helpless. He didn't even grunt when she landed a kick to his shin.

The combination of her arousal, anger and fear only served to excite him further, which was plain to see as her eyes strayed to his heavy erection. She panted with the force of her efforts, and soon he panted with her but for different reasons.

The man moved his head in a reptilian way, swift and graceful, and his mouth worked as if savoring the last flavors of her blood on his tongue. "I have tasted you now, beauty. We shall never again be apart." His breathing was harsh and his nostrils flared.

The look of dark, raw possession that blazed from his inhuman eyes seared through her, branding her as his. A second later she fell into the darkness that came and swallowed her up like the cold maw of a grave.

Morrigan shot upright in her bed.

Her rapid breaths ravaged her lungs. Her heart thundered in her chest. With shaking hands she turned on the bedside lamp and cast her panicked gaze about the room. Foolish as it sounded she was searching for monsters hidden in the shadows. Her fear in the dream had left a lingering, bitter taste in her mouth. She moaned brokenly as she buried her face into her hands.

After a few deep, calming breaths, she laughed shakily. In her mind she knew the dreams weren't real and that her fears were foolish, but her heart was still thundering in her chest. She rose from the bed and padded across the thick rugs covering the cold floor, heading to the bathroom for a drink of water.

Fingers fumbling and clumsy, she turned on the light and approached the sink. Catching sight of herself in the vanity she cried out in shock.

Two

JEWEL GREEN EYES stared back from her reflection, dark and haunted with all they had seen. Her usually peaches and cream complexion was pale and translucent in the harsh light. Wild tangled waves made a halo of her hair, which had escaped the tight braid she always wore to bed.

She hastily splashed water against her face. Making a cup of her hands she drank greedily, washing away the coppery taste of fear and blood from her dream. Her hands brushed against her lower lip and she winced in pain. Suddenly she fell still and after a few frantic heartbeats she slowly lowered her hands away from her face.

Her eyes were wide with shock. The look within them approached terror as she studied the inner lining of her lip. Seeing as well as feeling the small cut there, she let loose a high-pitched giggle. The cut was fresh though the bleeding had stopped. For a split second she feared that her dream was real before she laughed again and pushed the thought desperately away.

She wasn't crazy. The dreams, though realistic, were not real. The wound on her lip had likely occurred from biting her lip in her sleep while tossing and turning in the sheets. The memories of her dream, while frightening and consuming, should be forgotten upon waking.

Clinging to her mantra, she crawled back into bed. Snuggling down into the covers with near desperation, she shuddered from the cold of the night. It was almost an hour before she went back to sleep. She left the light on.

Morning arrived, and the rising sun greeted Morrigan as she stood on her balcony. The crisp dawn air made her skin clammy. Sipping from her steaming mug of coffee, she stared dazedly off into the distance. Her last hours of sleep had been restless ones, consumed by yet another dream. If something didn't change soon she was going to break down completely.

She was so tired.

This last dream had been so real—so much more than a nightmare. It had consumed her utterly, staying with her long after she'd left her bed and sleep behind. This last dream had taken place—not in the woods as so many had in the past—but in the dining room of her new house.

The man had been seated at the long table in her dining room, eating red berries from a bowl. Their crimson juices stained his mouth, just as her blood had in her earlier dream. His iridescent wings lay like a cape behind the back of his chair. Purple eyes blazed beneath the sweeping, wavy locks of his black hair, looking at her steadily as she stood there in a scarlet velvet gown that fell to the floor.

Even in her dreams she had excellent taste in clothing.

Obeying some unspoken command she walked forward, closer to where her dream man sat waiting. The heavy gown's long train dragged at her, holding her back like a desperate hand. But as much as she wanted to run, she was compelled to move closer. The man's lips twisted with a small, dark smile, as if he knew her dilemma.

He was completely nude, as always. Even struggling as she was against the sensual lure, she was forced to admit how erotic and perfect a male specimen he was. Sexy and dangerous, he lorded over the dining room like a king. Power and control oozed from his every pore, making her feel like a hag in his presence.

He offered her one of the strangely shaped berries with a graceful flourish. "Taste of their nectar, my beauty," he said in his haunting, lyrical voice. Rain pelted against the high paned windows, saturating the air with the scent of ozone and ocean. Bright flashes from occasional streaks of lightning illuminated his pale skin so that it was awash in a silver brilliance that blinded her.

Morrigan felt the overwhelming compulsion that accompanied his command. The last steps that brought her to his side were faltering ones, but she could not resist his powerful lure. With shaking hands she reached out to take the fruit from his strong fingers.

He pulled back from her and shook his head slightly. With the small movement his dark curls brushed over his wings and they stirred slightly. Offering the fruit once more, his eyes blazed at her with a wicked promise. "Feed from my hand, or not at all," he commanded. His voice echoed around the room and in the darkest corners of her mind.

What choice did she have but to obey such a forceful command? She was weary of fighting his pull on her—his will was so much stronger than her own. The fruit certainly looked inviting, and she was very hungry.

Dipping from the waist in an almost formal gesture, she sank her teeth into the succulent flesh of the berry. Her lips brushed his fingers with an electric jolt. Her vision dimmed and swam drunkenly. The world tilted, taking her with it.

How much time passed, she didn't know, but she came to with a dreamy reluctance. She was sitting on his lap, and as he held her steady with one hand she drank greedily from the other as he held it to her lips. Scarlet liquid pooled in her mouth as she drew upon a wound in his wrist. Visions assailed her. Sights of unimaginable wonder flooded her mind as she swallowed each heady draught.

Her mouth was full of the spicy sweet flavor of his blood, and she drew deeply from him once more before at last coming to her full senses. In desperation she wrenched her body from his embrace, trembling and shaking as she fell to the floor.

A wild and tangy bouquet rested on her tongue. This last mouthful of his blood was sweet, rich, and intoxicating. Resisting the urge to swallow the potent elixir, she made to spit it out upon the floor.

The man moved with a speed she couldn't follow with her eyes. One moment he sat calmly, the next he crouched before her. His hand laid over her mouth, gentle but immovable, preventing her from expelling his blood. Eyes wild, she struggled to pull away, but he was far too strong and held her firm.

"No, my beauty, swallow it down. Swallow every last drop and drink it deep. This is my essence—it will bond me to you—and you will not spit it out."

Morrigan shook her head against his hand. The blood burned yet tasted sweet in her mouth. His hand held her firm, and the look in his eyes effectively stilled her protests. With a sudden movement he brought her body flush against his.

His naked flesh seared her through the dress. He laid her back with a swift movement, and rested atop her. In this new position her struggles disappeared except for the refusal to swallow his blood.

The delicious feel of his weight anchored her. The other hand that held her rose to close his fingers gently around her nostrils, cutting off her air supply. Moments passed as their wills battled, purple eyes boring into hers. Her vision swam and she began to see spots. When she thrashed against him he merely settled between her legs, giving her proof of how her struggles only served to excite him in the evidence of his erection.

It was inevitable, with no air to breathe, that she would swallow his blood in a reflexive action. Immediately he allowed her the use of her lungs once more. He tenderly trailed a hand through her hair. His body snuggled down upon her, and he burrowed his lips against her throat in a heated kiss that let her feel the sharp press of his fangs . . .

The dream had ended, and Morrigan had once more bolted upright in her bed. Outside her bedroom terrace, a gentle rain beat against the house, and her mouth had been filled with the wild flavor of the dream. She'd bitten her lip again, staining her teeth a crimson she'd immediately brushed away.

She'd been far too frightened to go back to sleep, preferring instead to wait for dawn with the aide of caffeine. Feeling lost and lonely and deeply frightened of the increasing frequency of her dreams, she'd called a friend in New York. Leaving a message on her answering machine when there was no reply, Morrigan sat back and brooded.

The sun was high when the phone rang shrilly, breaking the quiet and making Morrigan jump. She raced to reach the phone on her bedside table, heart racing.

"Hello?"

"Are you alright, hon? I just got your message—long night out, ya know?"

"Oh Veronica, I'm so glad to hear your voice. I'm fine now that you've called. How's Ronnie the Actor working out?"

"Girl, you're a week behind the times. I'm with Navarre the Designer now. Are you sure you're all right? You sound odd."

"I'm just tired. Traveling has me lagging," she laughed, and even to her own ears it sounded a little crazy.

"Sounds like more than the traveling—you sound terrible. No offense, doll, but it's true."

"Well, you know, I'm just having trouble sleeping with all these changes—"

"You're not still having those damn nightmares are you? I *told* you moving and leaving your life behind wouldn't change that. You just need some strong meds, a weeklong Caribbean cruise, and a lover with lots of stamina."

"I don't want to end up dependent on drugs and sex like half of the people I know."

"Like me, you mean," Veronica's voice was flat.

"No! It's—that's not what I meant," she sighed. "It's just that I want to get through this problem without causing a bunch of other ones. I *needed* this change, Veronica. I wish you would understand that."

"Oh, I understand you felt trapped here. I understand you felt that fame was just too much for you. But *Scotland*? When you said you wanted to move closer to the water I thought maybe you meant Florida or California—someplace warm and happy. But just look at you—you picked someplace cold and the water there is black and icky, not blue."

"I think I'll like it here. The land is wild and inspiring—just the right place for a poet."

"You left all that behind, remember?"

"I'll always be a poet, Veronica. Poetry's in my blood. I just won't write for money so much as pleasure now." She smiled at the thought.

"I think you're crazy to give up the showbiz life. You can never have too much money, and if you enjoy writing why not get paid for it? You know what I think? I think you'll be back here in six months—you're too smart to leave the fame and glory behind you like this."

"Well I certainly hope you're wrong. I'm ready to settle down and live my life for myself. I have more than enough money to live in the lap of luxury until my old age—longer if I'm careful. I never wanted fame and the stress of a high-profile life. I think I'll be happy here."

"Well you certainly seem to have found just as much stress there as you did here. Look at you, in less than three months you've moved to a different country, retired from the music biz, and separated yourself from all your friends. But all that did was give you a new environment to worry in—and a lonelier one at that.

"You need to come back home, where the surroundings and people are familiar. Your insomnia and nightmares and all that will go away in no time, and then you can get back to business as usual."

Had she really thought anyone would understand or sympathize? Now, hearing all the same worn out lectures coming from the mouth of her closest friend, she wasn't sure why she'd even bothered calling in the first place. She would conquer these nightmares herself and be the stronger for it, it was that simple. It had to be.

Veronica's words were still streaming in her ear. "I don't even know why you're so freaked out about these dreams in the first place. You can bet that if I dreamed of some drop-dead gorgeous hunk like your dream guy, I'd be all over him like white on rice. The next time you dream of him you should just jump his bones and get it over with. I bet that will turn those dreams from nightmares into fantasies in a heartbeat. Before long you'll be looking forward to them."

"You don't understand, Veronica. These dreams aren't like that—this *man* isn't like that. He's dangerous and the things that happen in the dreams are dangerous. When they're going on all I can think to do is run away."

"It's just a Freudian thing. What does he do? He lives by the water and you run to him. These are probably just mental projections of your insecurities or whatever—I'm sure your therapist went over it with you."

"But they're different now. He's a vampire now, or . . . or *something*. Complete with fangs and wings and hungry appetites. I know it's screwy but these dreams seem so real I feel like I've lost touch with reality every time I wake up."

"Then maybe I was more right than you know about needing a young stud. Sounds to me like you're just horny—and that his fangs represent a penis and his wings represent you spreading your legs and 'taking flight,' so to speak."

Morrigan laughed despite herself. "That's the most retarded thing I've ever heard you say. I think his *erection* in every dream represents a penis and the rest are just a bunch of nightmare visions because I'm still suffering from all the same worries."

"Listen, girlfriend. I know it may not seem like it, but I just want you to be happy. I can't understand how you'll find happiness out there in that cold, craggy country, but I hope that you do. I'll never understand how you could just walk away from the high-life but I'll try not to judge you too harshly."

"I appreciate that, Veronica, I really do. If it's any consolation, this wasn't an easy thing for me to do. But it had to be done or I would have just lost it completely. I couldn't live in the spotlight any longer. I felt like a specimen under a microscope. It wasn't healthy for me."

"Just remember that if you want to come back, don't let your pride keep you from it. You'll always have a place here."

Morrigan wondered if Veronica would say the same in six months. The entertainment industry had a very short attention span . . . it was something she was especially counting on with this move. She'd just never given much thought about how many friends she would lose along the way.

"Thanks, Veronica. I'll keep all that in mind, I promise."

The two women said their goodbyes. Morrigan knew that it would probably be the last goodbye between them.

Three

LATER THAT SAME afternoon as Morrigan finished with the last of her unpacking, she was suddenly consumed with the urge to walk the grounds of her new property. She donned her best hiking boots, rattiest jeans, and sweatshirt before heading out the back door. As she walked through the back yard her copper braid glinted in the sunlight.

Despite the cool weather, she soon warmed up from her exertions. Her footsteps carried her beyond the yard into the wooded forest beyond. A tiny animal pathway led her deeper into the sheltering trees, though she was careful to keep her home within sight. As unfamiliar as she was with the terrain, she didn't want to risk getting lost in the dense thicket of trees.

After several moments of walking, she felt sealed off from the outside world completely. Here the forest coverage had thickened, shielding her from the sunshine. Twilight shadows played all about. It was cooler here away from the sun, and she shivered.

The singsong of wild birds and the rustle of ground dwelling animals faded slowly into silence. The only sound that broke through the wood was the muffled footfalls of her feet as she trudged through the underbrush.

Morrigan looked around at the trees and shrubberies, breathing deeply of the crisp forest air. For the first time in months she began to feel a real sense of calm and peace overtake her. She'd made the right choice in moving here, she decided with a tiny smile. Despite everyone's warnings to the contrary her coming here was exactly what she needed.

If ever there was a place to rediscover herself, this was it.

Whether or not this place would become her true home remained to be seen. But deep down she knew this was the right place at the right time for . . . whatever it was she was seeking. After only two short days she felt more at ease—happier—than she'd ever felt in her native New York. Whatever compulsion had driven her to come to this foreign land, she was glad of it. She was glad to be here.

Spotting a moss-covered log, she sat and surveyed her surroundings with an appreciative eye. It was dark here in the heart of the forest, twilight-blue and soothing. A few stray shards of sunlight cut through the thick overhead canopy to reach the woodland floor. It lent a fairy tale quality to the land.

Morrigan could almost imagine tiny fairies and gnomes traveling through the wood and she chuckled. Surely in all the world this was a place of magic and wonder. It was the perfect place for a creative soul to thrive and prosper.

Smells of growing things, rich soils, and moist bark assailed her nostrils, along with the tangy ozone smell of crisp flowing water. Looking around she could see no sign of a stream or loch, though there was probably one very close by. Idly she wondered how far she had strayed from the house, realizing just how long it had been since she'd lost visibility of the backyard.

Suddenly she grew tense. Nervous now, she hastily made to rise from her perch upon the fallen log.

Strong, cool hands clamped firmly onto her shoulders. The smell of rain and rushing water was stronger now. Silky, midnight black curls fell over her shoulders as the man behind her leaned down to whisper in her ear.

"Don't go just yet."

Morrigan let loose a strangled cry and tried to rise from the log once more. To her dismay the man would not release his hold on her. She was forced to stay seated, and though he was strong enough to hold her still, he was gentle and did not bruise her.

Her heart shuddered in her breast and her lips quivered with a giddy fear. "God, I'm going crazy. I'm going crazy," she rasped. Her harsh breathing seemed to boom in the thick silence around them.

"Shh, no my beauty, never think so. Try to calm yourself. I can taste your fear and smell it on the wind. I do not wish for you to fear me. Never that."

Morrigan wasn't listening to his words, but the tone of his voice soothed her as nothing else could. His dulcet tones echoed in her mind, sending a deep thrum of calm washing through her body. Soon her heart rate slowed until it was almost normal, and her panicked breaths eased their cadence as she calmed.

A dreamy languor overtook her, and she involuntarily leaned back against him. Her head fell to the side, resting against his arm at her shoulder. Several moments passed in silence, her eyes lazy and hooded as she came close to dozing off.

Without breaking contact with her reclining back, the man moved lower to crouch behind her. Her head fell back further to rest upon his shoulder, exposing her neck fully to him. The cool touch of his lips upon her throat didn't even shock her, she was so completely at ease. Like the softest whispering caress he pressed a kiss against the beat of her pulse, darting his tongue out to taste her.

Licking and laving her there, his tongue seemed so much hotter than his lips. He seemed to brand her. He growled softly, pressing more firmly against her, letting her feel the points of his teeth. Whatever dark enchantment held her quiet wavered for a moment and she felt a frisson of her earlier fear creep back.

"Please don't," she managed.

"But I must, beauty. The memory of the taste—the feel and smell of you—has haunted me. The spice and sweetness of you lingers upon my senses. I must taste of you again. No mere memory can last me long enough to sustain my hunger for you."

"Don't," she choked out as he dipped his head to press another hot kiss against her pulse.

His words were muffled against her flesh. "Don't fight this. Feel only the pleasure of it—the rightness of it." The power of his musical voice ensorcelled her once more. Thankfully it eased the panic that tried to overtake her.

As he licked her again, a long wet trail along her neck, she felt his teeth trace lightly over her flesh once more. This time she didn't fear it. Instead, a wave of lust so raw and strong swept through her, making her gasp. Heat pooled low in her belly, making her weak against him. A quiet, breathy moan escaped her lips, and she arched her neck more fully to his kiss.

"Yes," he breathed. "You feel the heat and strength of our bond, don't you? I can smell your arousal. It's such a delicious perfume." His hands tightened on her convulsively.

"You make me want you so much." He murmured something else, something dark and erotic sounding but she couldn't make out the words.

His hands moved down from her shoulders to cup her breasts lovingly, kneading them until they felt swollen and achy. Thumbs teased her nipples to excited points through the thick cotton of her sweatshirt. He rolled her nipples between his thumb and forefingers, the friction of his movements setting her body aflame with awakened desire.

Panting softly, she arched her back wantonly, sending her breasts more firmly into his skilled and knowing hands. Her thighs parted of their own accord and immediately his hand cupped the intimate flesh between them. He rubbed her there, putting exquisite pressure upon her swollen clit through the fabric of her jeans and causing her to tremble with need.

The heated kisses at her neck were demanding and she felt his mouth open wide against her. He sank his fangs deeply into the pulsing vein at her neck, growling low in his throat. There was no pain, only a huge wave of pleasure that threatened to drown her in its intensity. She was thrust straight into the arms of a violent orgasm.

In the back of her dazed mind she was stunned at her reaction to him. He was drinking her blood and she was reveling in it like a wanton. Exquisite claws of ecstasy raked down her body, causing her to shudder and writhe, but her mind raced to try and regain control of her traitorous emotions. It was useless, she was in thrall to the pleasure he gave her so freely and unreservedly. She was lost.

The pulsing heat of her ecstasy radiated outward from his deeply embedded fangs. It flooded down through her breasts and straight to her womb. She screamed with her release, rotating her hips against his manipulating hand. He drew deep from her vein, his jaw working against her like a child suckling its mother. The more he drank from her the harder she came.

With a sudden unexpected movement, he pulled back from her. His tongue swept along the wound as his fangs withdrew from her flesh. That lingering caress caused such a clenching in her womb that her whole body jerked and almost unseated her. The wind was a sudden chill against her neck as he left her, and her orgasm slowly subsided, leaving her weak and spent. She lay boneless against him, shocked at her behavior. But she was too dazed from the pleasure to move away.

After a last, loving pat to her still tingling vagina, he moved. His hands took a firm hold to keep her upright and he came around to stand before her. His purple eyes gazed deeply into her own for a long heartbeat. Morrigan was the first to look away, as if she could make him disappear by not acknowledging his presence.

A hand at her chin moved her to face him, and he pressed his lips softly to hers. His lips were no longer cool. They were heated with the warmth of the blood he'd drunk from her. Strangely enough, as this thought surfaced it didn't alarm her. Rather, it sent a thrill of renewed desire coursing through her.

His mouth opened on hers, and she welcomed his tongue within, meeting its strokes with her own. The taste of him was wild and exciting, and the feel of his fangs against her lips made her thighs clench with erotic need. Her hands came up and encircled his neck as she lost herself in the kiss.

She should have been frightened by the strength of her response to this dream-man. For all she knew she had finally lost hold of the reins to her sanity. This seemed so *real*. Seeing the physical and very real manifestation of a winged vampire while awake was . . . insane. But she felt no fear, and no panic—not now.

Now, in his arms, she felt only pleasure and acceptance within herself. She gladly gave in to the wondrous feelings that wanted to consume and overwhelm her. Eager and excited, she kissed him with a hunger and fervor to match his own, leaning against his naked flesh.

Fangs nipped gently at her lips, before he bit down upon his own tongue, drawing blood. He thrust his tongue and his blood into her mouth. His strong hands moved to her head, holding her captive. Their tongues dueled, and her mouth flooded with the sweet warmth of his blood.

Not stopping to think, not even giving herself time to fear him, she suckled greedily on his tongue. The wetness of his blood smeared their meshed lips as he bled freely into her. She swallowed every precious drop he fed to her.

She was insatiable.

Her body was flooded with the taste, smell and feel of him. It intoxicated her, this primal feeding, and her vision swam beneath her closed lids. Her world burned with the purple fire borne from his eyes, and she lost all sense of time and place, giving herself over to his dark desires.

She came back to herself slowly, moments—maybe hours—later, when he moaned against her mouth with the force of his own orgasm. It was obvious he too found pleasure when she drank his blood. She reached out and felt his semen spill hot and wet over her hand. Stroking his powerful cock as it pulsed in her hand, she was humbled by the raw magic of the moment. His moan of release hummed against her mouth and into her throat as he moved, thrusting in her hand.

In that moment she felt complete. With her hand awash with

his seed and her mouth full of the taste of him, she felt as if she'd come home. She wanted him so badly that she ached, and had he asked it of her she would gladly have given him anything—*everything*. It was madness.

He pulled reluctantly from their kiss, nipping her lips before he drew free of her. He cleaned his sperm from her hand with some fallen leaves before he swept his hand through her hair. Dislodging her braid he tangled his fist within the copper waves. Movement was impossible as he held her with his hand and with his eyes. "Morrigan, my beauty, do you know me now?"

Visions assailed her, and she swam in the deep purple ocean of his gaze. With a sudden, startling clarity she *did* know him. "Azure," her voice faltered, hoarse with emotion. "Your name is Azure, but you are called Az by your friends and family."

A blinding, fanged smile was her reward, and he pressed a soft kiss to her brow. He gathered her more closely to him, this new embrace a comfort where the others had been arousing. She returned the embrace, in thrall to the magic of the moment. It was a moment of discovery and revelation. How did she know his name? How could she know that he had been searching for her—his mate—for years, and that he'd almost given up hope of ever finding her?

In those moments it didn't matter how she knew. It didn't matter that this was likely a dream, or hallucination. Running her hands lovingly down the silky soft cape of his wings, she sighed and rested against him. She felt so right, so content as he held her. There was no room for fear.

Az pulled away from her and held her upper arms in a firm yet gentle grip. "You will no longer fear me, Morrigan, my beauty. You will welcome me into your dreams and dread them no more."

The reminder of her dreams, spoken aloud like this, made her shy away. He held her firm. "I have not the strength to meet you above water like this, in your waking hours, very often. Your dreams are an easier meeting place for you and I until I am at my full strength. I will visit you there with greater ease now that we have shared blood. We are bonded now, and soon we can be together for all eternity. But for now, I must return to the water."

Morrigan felt dazed as he helped her to stand. He pressed a heated kiss to her palm, and with a small gust of wind he disappeared before her very eyes. The abruptness of his departure, coupled with her blood loss, served as her undoing.

With a tiny expulsion of air her eyes rolled upwards into the back of her head. She fell to the ground in a dead faint.

four

THE CLOCK STRUCK midnight and Morrigan jumped in her chair with a startled shriek. In one hand she held an aluminum baseball bat, while with the other she reached for yet another cup of coffee that sat cooling at her side. She huddled in her den before a roaring fire, feet curled up beneath her on the plush recliner as she fought against sleep.

Sleep was her enemy now.

In her mind she knew it was beyond foolish to think she could avoid sleep forever, but she fought against it anyway. Her nerves were jumping from the excess of caffeine she'd imbibed, but at this point she didn't know what else to do—she feared sleeping more than anything now.

It would probably be wisest for her now if she sought medical help. But she couldn't risk going to the hospital for treatment right away because the ensuing publicity was sure to ruin any chances she had for peace in her new home. It was too soon after her public retirement to risk drawing attention to herself. The media would have a field day.

But she obviously couldn't cope with her mental state on her own. Especially not after the newest developments of this hysteria. Whatever the causes for her hallucinations, they hadn't been solved by her recent change in lifestyle. If anything, they had grown much worse.

Morrigan had no idea what was happening to her anymore. After waking up in the woods at sunset, she had walked home. Strangely enough she'd been calm and at ease. Her mind had been blessedly blank. It hadn't been until much later that she had discovered the tender bruise at her neck.

It was then that reality had come crashing down on her.

Looking in the mirror she couldn't deny the evidence of two faintly bruised puncture wounds marring her skin. What on earth was happening to her? The lines between dream and reality were blurring in her mind. Her thoughts were a confused muddle. The wounds on her neck were real—how anything but a set of very sharp fangs caused them she couldn't say. There were no rational explanations.

Were the overwhelming, erotic visions of Az real? But that would be impossible—the man wasn't even human. *Obviously*. He sported fangs and wings, and he drank blood. Her blood! In addition, there was no way that she'd willingly have drunk his blood. Not unless it was a dream or hallucination. *Right*?

Right.

Perhaps if she repeated these things over and over in her head, it would make them so . . . but in the meantime she refused to fall asleep. Az had promised to see her in her dreams. She refused to give him the chance. She had to be careful not to give him an opportunity to consume her so fully again, as he had this afternoon in the forest.

Bah! Az—she was thinking of him as though he was real and not a figment of her overstressed imagination. He was a fairy tale monster from the dredges of her subconscious, right? A demon or monster, come to torment her with nightmare visions of drinking blood.

Sure, she'd enjoyed every moment of it. But that was crazy, right? No sane person would find pleasure in such dark visions.

Why did her body pulse with the remembered pleasure of his embrace? Why could she not stop thinking about his beauty and power? How his voice wrapped around her like cool silken sheets, and how sensual was his kiss. She didn't know why, and didn't care to. For now it was enough that she had some small will remaining that was her own.

She would fight this dream man's stranglehold on her body and emotions. Refusing to fall asleep tonight was the safest course that she could see. So she would stay here, huddled before the fire, grasping the only weapon she could find as though it were a lifeline.

Draining her mug, wincing against the heat of the coffee as it burned her throat, she blinked furiously. It was difficult not to become hypnotized by the golden dance of the flames before her. Her eyes were heavy lidded and burning from lack of rest. It had been days since she'd had any peaceful sleep. The dreams of Az had been haunting her with increasing frequency, and she knew that if she slept now he would already be there waiting for her.

The thought both frightened and thrilled her. She didn't understand herself anymore.

The hours of the night stretched on, and she worked to find things to occupy her weary mind. She switched on the television, tried to write some poetry, and even went so far as to take a cold shower. The shock sent her muscles screaming, but it did wake her up enough that she gained a solid hour of wakefulness without having to fight for it.

But sleep would not be staved off for very long. Her sleepless nights were catching up to her all at once, and there wasn't much she could do about it. Her body was trembling with fatigue. She knew it was only a matter of time now.

As dawn painted the horizon with hues of violet and tangerine, she at last gave in. She fell asleep, sitting upright in her chair as the television droned on to break the silence. Her baseball bat fell unnoticed to the floor, and her head slumped to the side.

All her dreams left her blessedly alone. Either she was too tired to dream or too comforted by the daylight. It didn't really matter. She slept peacefully, long into the day.

It was almost four o'clock when Morrigan at last awakened. She stretched. Her body was cramped from sitting slumped in the chair for so long. Her neck and spine popped audibly, but despite her aches and pains she felt deliciously well rested. She smiled as she rose from her makeshift bed.

"No dreams, thank God," she said aloud to herself. She hoped they were over at last. She hoped she had exorcised them from her subconscious mind with yesterday's culminating hallucination. Something had to give because she couldn't keep living like this—in fear of sleep, in fear of dreams.

Forcefully she pushed her musings aside. Such wonderings would get her nowhere. They would serve only to upset her. Her stomach growled and she went to the kitchen in search of food. Looking through the refrigerator and in her cupboards—both fully stocked by her housekeeping service the day before her arrival—she found to her disgust that nothing appealed to her.

Nothing looked appetizing though her stomach burned with unappeased hunger, making its discontent known with noisy gur-

gles. Nausea assailed her when she tried to eat some salted crackers. She feared she might be coming down with a flu bug. With as
little rest as she was getting, it would be no wonder if she got sick
on top of things.

In one of her cupboards she spotted a can of tomato soup and
realized with surprise that the thought of eating it was quite agree-
able to her queasy stomach. She *hated* plain tomato soup—never
ate the stuff unless it was used as an ingredient for something else.

It was odd.

Oh well, better the soup than nothing at all. And right now her
stomach didn't want anything but the soup. She went out onto the
backyard veranda to consume her bounty of tomato soup and red
wine. Surprisingly it was quite palatable and she had no trouble
keeping it down.

"Well, that wasn't so bad," she said to break the silence. Her
stomach was full, her mind and body well rested. What more
could anyone ask for? With a lighter heart she cleaned up the rem-
nants of her meal and went inside to write.

All the while she prayed that her waking dream of the day before would not come to intrude on her today.

five

LATER THAT SAME night, Morrigan ran a hot bath for herself in her master bathroom. The huge sunken tub in the center of the large room was made of solid marble and was big enough for four people to recline in easily. It was one of the main reasons she'd so desired to buy the house. She loved the water and enjoyed a relaxing soak in a long hot bath.

She added scented bubbles and lit tapers and tea candles all around the rim of the giant tub. With no other light source, the room flickered with dancing shadows cast by the flames. The steaming water sparkled where the bubbles parted to allow a peek at the liquid beneath.

Removing her floor length robe of blue satin, she stepped into the welcoming bathwater. Her hair was loose and when her body had adjusted to the temperature of the water, she ducked her head below the surface to saturate it. She washed her hair and body until she shone with a rosy glow.

Leaning back she let the dance of the candles' flames lull her. Her eyes grew heavy in the rising steam, and her breathing slowed. It had been so long since she'd been this relaxed. Well, aside from those moments after her orgasm in Az's arms yesterday.

But that had been a dream and this was reality, and she felt totally relaxed for the first time in ages.

Sleep overtook her swiftly, too quickly for her to fight against it. One moment she was awake—the next she was in her dream state. That quickly the scene changed and she stood nude before the sunken tub. Within it Az reclined lazily, waiting for her.

The water was full of floating crimson rose petals. So full, in fact, that the water was as dark and thick as blood. The black curls of Az's hair were like a patch of deep midnight, not even reflecting the glow of the thousands of surrounding candles.

His normally pale skin was golden in the light and his muscular chest rose above the waterline. He raised a hand from the depths of the dark water and held it out to her, beckoning her closer.

"Come and join me, sweet Morrigan. I hunger for your . . . touch."

Without thinking twice, her earlier fears of an encounter with him forgotten, she moved into the aromatic crimson water. She sighed in bliss as the water lapped at her hips and waist. She smiled and took his outstretched hand with her own. His skin was cool and strangely dry despite the water.

She'd noticed this about him before. He never seemed to get wet. She was moved to remark on it.

"You're never dripping when you come from the water. Not even your hair gets wet." Even to her own ears her voice was throaty from her rising passions.

Az smiled, his eyes roving appreciatively over her breasts as they bobbed in the water. His hungry gaze was hot enough to burn her. Instinctively her body reacted to the promise held in his purple gaze.

He spoke in that beautiful voice she so loved to hear. "My body is different from yours. I have to move swiftly through the water and would be impeded if the water soaked into me—it would weigh me down. So my skin and hair stay dry even when I'm submerged. All of my kind is like this. But your skin," he drew in a deep breath, "glistens beautifully with the water. It shines like a mirror, or a star. It makes me thirst to sip the water from your flesh."

That dark voice washed over and through her. It sent heat pooling low within her belly. Her vagina clenched and flooded with wet, silken warmth that had nothing to do with the water surrounding them. The air trembled with her shuddering breaths. Ripples in the water moved around her breasts, drawing his eyes there once again.

He reached out and laid a hand upon an already erect nipple. His skin, as always, was a cool contrast against the heat of hers. The sensation only heightened the pleasure of his touch. Her nipple swelled almost painfully and he eased it with a swipe of his thumb.

"What are you?"

"Would it ease your fears somewhat if I told you?"

"You're not human," she dodged the question. Her fears *were* creeping up on her—how could he know?

"I can smell your fear," he answered her unspoken question. "Perhaps you're not ready to know."

"I have to know. I'm going crazy and I need some answers."

"You're not going crazy," he emphasized. "I'll tell you what I am if it will help to ease your worries. I am not from your world. I'm not a human—though you've already guessed that much. I am from a race called Icari. My world is far from here, past many stars and galaxies."

"How did you get here?"

"Through gateways in the water of our worlds, portals through space. I have come far, through many such portals, to find you."

41

Morrigan swallowed harshly and tried to concentrate more on his words than on the light caresses of his hand upon her breast. His fingers plucked idly at her nipple, as if he was unaware of his actions or their effect upon her. Her body sang with pleasure that radiated from his every touch. It was very hard to keep her mind on the conversation.

"W-why were you looking for me?"

"Can you not guess that much? Will you deny even that small admission to yourself and to me?" His voice had grown hard with the last words.

Looking deeply into his glowing eyes she shied away from the truth she found within them.

"Yes. You *know*. You are my mate, my woman."

"I don't believe you."

"Yes you do. Lying will not change the truth."

"I don't believe in such things."

"You don't believe in destiny? In love and in passion?" His voice was chiding.

"You're not real! You're a figment of my overstressed imagination, and easily treatable with medication." She scrunched up her eyes and shook her head back and forth. She wouldn't—couldn't let this dream get out of hand.

"How many times have you said that to yourself? And how many times have you awakened to find proof that these aren't mere dreams? We were destined for each other. It's an instinctive bond we both share—though you fight against it now. I've come to claim you, as is my right by the laws of Fate.

"If it's reassurance you seek, that I can give to you and gladly. I swear that I will pleasure your body, your mind and your soul, in ways you can't even begin to imagine. I will turn you inside out and make you scream with ecstasy the likes of which you have never known. You have never known joy and happiness the likes of which I can give you.

"I will keep you safe from harm. I will love and worship you all my days. Whatever you ask for, I will give it and gladly. You know the truth of my words, deep down, even though you stubbornly fight against it."

"Why are you saying these things?" she couldn't help asking.

His eyes blazed. "Because I mean them. Because for years I've been alone. Now I've found you . . . and I'm not letting you go." His words echoed darkly in the candlelit room, thrilling and frightening her with their intensity. He bent his head and his breath fanned hotly over her parted lips.

"I'm keeping you," he said, before he swooped down like a bird of prey and claimed her lips in a soul-stirring kiss.

Morrigan kissed him back with a fervor she hadn't known she possessed. He dug his hands into the flesh of her hips and drew her closer to him, lifting her and settling her legs astride his own. He pulled the wet heat of her into shocking, sudden contact with his rock-hard shaft.

She gasped as the muscles of her vagina clenched greedily, setting her already swollen clit to pulsing against the heavy weight of his cock. As he kissed her his fangs scraped her tender lips. She moved against him wantonly. Never before had she felt such a consuming hunger, never felt so wet or ready for sex as she did now.

Her body was trembling with the force of her desire, and she couldn't understand it. She knew she should be fighting this, frightened out of her wits—but she wasn't afraid at all. Not anymore. Reality could come later, but for now she wanted to lose herself in his arms. Admittedly it was what she'd always wanted from the first.

Az sent his seeking mouth down to her breast and slurped a straining nipple into his mouth. She moaned aloud at the caress. His mouth was so much hotter than the rest of him, and it scalded her with its dark eroticism. Her vaginal muscles contracted and tingled as his penis brushed against her clit.

She wondered how it would feel to orgasm around his cock.

Freeing her nipple with a wet popping sound, he moved on to the other one, his fangs scraping against her in his ardor. She gasped at the small pain and moaned when he soothed it with his tongue. Her head was thrown back and his arm supported her back as it bowed. They moaned and sighed. They were both lost in the heat of the moment.

Growling, he turned with her in the water. Pulling her beneath him, he took them both beneath the water. They surfaced, with Morrigan sputtering her surprise, their hair and skin awash with red rose petals. He grinned wickedly, flashing his fangs. With strong hands he lifted her up to lie propped against the rim of the tub. She was splayed out before him, vulnerable, with her back arched and her breasts uplifted for his convenience. She glanced down at him, eyes wide, and watched him as he bathed her body with his lips, teeth and tongue.

Kissing each breast one last time he trailed his lips downward across her ribs and stomach. He dipped his tongue into the dark hollow of her navel, making her gasp and moan with his ardent attentions. In reward for her abandoned response he gently nipped at her flesh with the tips of his fangs. One solitary drop of blood appeared on her flesh.

He licked it away with his long, velvet tongue.

The image of his blatantly erotic tongue lapping against her flesh sent a pulse of raw lust raging through her body. He moved lower, and lower still, spreading her legs as wide as they would go with the immense breadth of his muscular shoulders.

Morrigan was given only a moment's warning as his blazing eyes met hers, before he dipped his head to lick her glistening, swollen clit. Velvet tongue lapping at her labia, he delved further to the hidden honey within. He moaned against her, the vibrations against her ultra-sensitive folds sending her soaring. Using his lips, teeth, and tongue mercilessly against her, he lapped at her juices. He drank deeply of her passionate response.

Morrigan threw back her head and arched more firmly against his devouring mouth. She drove her hands into his hair and pulled his face forcefully against her burning pussy, crying out as he ze-roed in knowingly upon her clit. When he suckled her there she undulated wildly against him. She came against his mouth with screaming abandon.

"God, God, I can't take it. Please . . . *I can't take anymore,*" she cried out brokenly as her orgasm spiraled ever onward, gaining in in-tensity with each draw of his lips against her clit. Her vaginal mus-cles clenched like a fist. She pulsed and quivered against his mouth.

Az thrust a long finger into her, twisting it into a hook to scrape that most magical place within her. Her body convulsed and the contractions of her orgasm renewed in their intensity. It felt as though her body were stretched out upon a rack of pleasure so in-tense it was close to pain.

She'd never felt so exquisitely alive.

Morrigan at last caught her breath and came down from that long, wicked dance in the heavens. She glanced out from beneath heavy lashes and caught sight of Az as he dipped his head to press a burning kiss to her inner thigh.

She could actually feel his hunger for her blood as if it were her own. She knew instinctively that he wished to feed from her. She wondered why he didn't move up over her and drink from her jugular as he had done before. She arched up against him, silently offering all that he desired, throwing herself on the altar of his pleasure.

Az looked up at her and Morrigan met his eyes steadily. His features were almost swallowed up by the amethyst blaze of his eyes. Never in her life had she seen a more erotic sight than his head there between her widely splayed legs.

She felt a renewed pulse of ecstasy radiate out from her core to the rest of her body. Her whole frame shuddered with the force of it. When his eyes strayed back to the flesh of her inner thigh, she knew what he wanted. Surprisingly, she wanted to give him all that he craved. And more.

"Please," she begged, shameless. "Feed from me, take all you want."

He needed no further urging and struck, sinking his teeth deeply into the flesh of her inner thigh. He drank deep of the hot, rich blood he drew there. Morrigan screamed with the force of another orgasm. It was unbelievable. She lost several moments as he fed there, his mouth drawing upon her voraciously. When she came back to herself she saw him positioning the tip of his thick erection between the lips of her glistening, wet flesh. His curly black hair shielded his face from her view and tickled teasingly against her belly.

She got a clear glimpse of his cock between the swaying locks of his hair and gasped with excitement. It was dark and engorged with blood, a long thick stalk—too thick for her to grasp her hand around him. The plum-shaped head slipped in her wetness as he moved into position, making her gasp with pleasure.

The massive head slipped into her slowly. It tightly stretched her flesh as it breached the mouth of her vagina. She was so wet he slid in with ease, and after a brief moment of resistance her body swallowed his cock greedily. He pushed it into her slowly, with ultimate care, as if afraid of hurting her if he moved too quickly.

Morrigan rose up and brought her lips to his. "I want it rough and hard," she said into his mouth.

Her words snapped the last threads of his control and he surged home. The thickness of his shaft invaded her, seating him deep. At last he came to rest with his sac slapping against her buttocks. The great head of his penis rested at the mouth of her womb.

Az's head was flung back, and the sight of his pleasure was the most moving thing Morrigan had ever seen. Slowly he moved out of her, his shaft coming almost free of her before surging back into her. Over and over he moved, tirelessly thrusting in and out of her. With every thrust and withdrawal she could feel his length moving through the whole of her body, reaching impossible depths. She'd never felt so invaded by a man before, and she loved it.

She moved against him, wanting more, and still more. All he had to give.

"Fuck me harder, Az," she begged shamelessly.

"Oh baby, *yes*," he said on a hissing growl before pummeling mercilessly into her.

Their bodies slapped against each other. The force of his thrusts made the water around them churn and splash. The wet sounds only served to inflame them further, and he pounded into her over and over. They splashed water over the rim of the tub, sending rose petals scattering around their straining bodies and across the floor beyond.

"God, I'm coming, *I'm coming again*," she screamed out in a voice that sounded nothing like her own.

"Come on, baby, milk me. Take it all," he said, fucking her so hard that his balls met her ass with an audible sound.

His words inflamed her, sending her spiraling over the peak of a violent climax the likes of which she'd never experienced. She screamed long and loud, writhing uncontrollably beneath his forcefully thrusting body.

Az threw back his head and let out a cry that sounded like the scream of a wild jungle cat. It echoed around the room as he burst within her. He bathed her womb in a gushing wave of hot cream. His cock pulsated over and over within her like the throb of a giant heartbeat.

They collapsed into each other's arms and lay spent, gasping, for several minutes. All was quiet but for the sound of their breathing. After some time had passed, Az pulled up from her, and looked deeply into her eyes. Concern and worry were written plainly on his face.

"I didn't feed you, baby. I'm sorry, forgive my rudeness. I was just too hot to have you and didn't think about it."

"I don't want to drink your blood, Az." Even though the memory of the taste of him was enough to make her hunger for more.

"You must feed, Morrigan, before you weaken from hunger and deprivation."

"I'm not hungry," she said and hoped that her stomach didn't growl and belie her words. "Besides, I can eat food when I get hungry. I don't need to drink blood to survive."

Az sent her a possessive look that thrilled her, even as his next words chilled her to the bone.

"You do now."

Six

"WHAT DO YOU mean?" she asked, knowing her tone had fallen flat in the wake of a sudden rush of fear.

"You know exactly what I mean."

"No, I don't. Tell me what you meant by that."

He sighed. "You have tasted of my blood, and I of yours. We are mates, and with the blood bond you are tied to me in all ways. You need my blood to survive or you'll grow weak.

"Today you must have noticed your distaste for normal food. Even so, I'll wager you hungered ravenously for sustenance. It was just your body adapting itself to the ways of an Icari. It's growing used to craving my blood. You can eat other foods, like the apriss fruit or sang-berries, but you need my blood to stay healthy."

Morrigan crawled backwards out of the tub to sit nude upon the wet floor. Her heated core rested on the wet, cool tiles. It was a reminder of her abandoned pleasure in his arms, even as her eyes flared wildly with renewed fright. "*Apriss fruit, or sang-berries*? I ate an entire can of tomato soup, that's pretty normal food for a human. How do you explain that?"

"Is this tomato soup red?"

"Y-yeah," she stuttered. "So what?"

"There's your explanation. You can ingest red foods, the closer to liquid form the better. You will crave only these red foods from now on. My people feed on such things as well. We have many to choose from—such as the apriss or sang-berry—they make up a large part of our diet. We don't merely live on blood, though that is what makes us the strongest. You'll grow used to it in time."

"I don't believe you!"

"Why are you denying this to yourself? You know I am right. Though I can see the knowledge frightens you, you need to come to terms with it soon. I know that you enjoy feeding from me, that you savor the taste of me. You are stronger when my essence fills and sustains you. How can that be a bad thing?"

"I'm not turning into some kind of alien vampire. I went out in the sun today. I ate solid food and I'm wearing a silver cross around my neck for God's sake!" Her voice rose higher and higher with her panic.

Az moved closer to her. Though he rose from the water, no drops of it clung to his skin. "We are not these vampires you so obviously fear, Morrigan. I have already told you our kind are Icari. We're water dwellers, not vampires. Please be calm." He reached out to lay a soothing hand upon her knee, but she crab-legged backwards away from him.

"Don't touch me!"

"It's too late for you to have these fears, Morrigan. Even now my seed is glistening on your flesh, proof enough for both of us that the time for misgivings is past. You enjoyed my touch. Why fight this one small thing?"

"Small thing? *Small thing?* You're telling me that I need to drink blood to survive and you call that a small thing?" Her voice rose to a shriek.

"Why are you so frightened? You enjoyed feeding on me. I enjoyed it too. How can you think something so beautiful and right could be bad?"

"I'm not like you. Wait—why am I even having this conversation? This is just a stupid dream. I just have to take control and wake up and everything will be fine. I have to wake up." She repeated it like a mantra, pinching the skin of her arms as if the pain would help her awaken.

"I will not let you leave this dream. Not until you are calmer. We have much to discuss, things you need to come to terms with before this dream ends," he said.

Morrigan glared at him. She ignored his words and continued to desperately chant, "Wake up . . . wake up."

"Be calm, my love. We can ease your fears together—" A strained, panicked look crossed his features. "No! Morrigan, you must quit fighting me. You're not ready to wake up."

His voice faded into nothingness.

Morrigan's eyes flew open only to find herself completely submerged beneath the bathwater. For a second she lay there, still beneath the calm surface. Then reality set it. She choked on a mouthful of water and shot upright in the tub.

"*God, what's wrong with me?*" she sobbed. Spitting up large amounts of water, she stumbled from the bathtub, her mind in a daze. She could have drowned. There was no telling how long she'd lain there beneath the surface of the water. The water was chilled, and the candles burned low . . . how long had she been asleep?

Naked, she ran to her bedroom in a panic. Already her hair and skin were drying—faster than she could have expected under the circumstances. She donned her clothing without bothering to towel off first. Before putting on a pair of skimpy panties she noticed the telltale fang marks on her inner thigh and sobbed anew.

It was too much. Was she crazy? Had her mind completely broken . . . or was Az real? At this particular moment she would almost have preferred being told she was crazy. It was better than having to face the idea of Az turning her into a bloodsucker. It was too much, too fast.

A warm wetness trickled down her thigh and she glanced at it. A purple, glowing liquid trailed lazily from beneath the silk of her thong. Instinctively she knew it was Az's semen. She shrieked as her panic reached critical mass and she hurriedly finished dressing. She felt her long hair streaming out behind her as she threw on a pair of running shoes and raced for the door.

Grabbing her car keys and purse as she fled, she jumped into her car and gunned the engine mercilessly. For a moment she paused, indecisive. What could she possibly accomplish by running away, after all? But staying here meant she would have to face her fear . . . and Az.

That was something she just wasn't ready to do. Tires squealed as she sped away. It felt as if she were leaving her heart behind. But she was too scared to wonder at it.

The pub was dimly lit and full of smoke when Morrigan walked in. Climbing into a shadowed booth, she ordered a Bloody Mary from a passing waitress. She tried to blend in with her surroundings. She wanted to fade into the background so that she wouldn't be noticed by anyone around her. What she needed was peace and quiet. She needed time to think.

For well over an hour she'd driven around. Aimlessly and in circles it seemed, until she'd finally made her way into the village proper. Spotting the pub in which she now found herself, her stomach had growled plaintively. It reminded her that she'd eaten very little all day.

Her mind had been racing since she'd fled her bath. She didn't know what to think about her situation. In her mind she'd already given up the illusion that the dreams were . . . well, *dreams*. If that made her crazy, then she no longer cared. Too many physical clues had stacked up, one on top of the other, for her to keep ignoring them.

From the beginning she'd been changing. Months ago, when she'd first dreamt of Az, she'd begun to feel . . . different. At first it was just her sudden wish to move nearer to the lochs of Scotland. Oh, she'd been planning for over a year to retire from the music business—but the decision to move out of the country had been a sudden one. Back then Az had just been a man reaching out to her from the heart of the water, an indistinct figure that had intrigued and frightened her. Right on the heels of those first dreams she'd seen the house in Meigle and purchased it on a whim.

She'd wanted to be closer to the water.

Since then the dreams had grown more consuming. More real. Az had stepped from the loch and claimed her with his kiss. He'd fed on her and she on him—binding them closer together than she could hope to understand at the time. The lines between her waking world and her dreaming world were blurred beyond her comprehension.

It was no longer feasible for her to ignore the physical signs that followed her into the waking world. Fang marks on her neck and thighs maybe once could have been excused as a scratch or insect bite. But more than that and she'd run out of explanations.

And the biggest kicker of all was the moist glow of his semen as it had dripped down her leg. There was no logical explanation for that. None at all, beyond the obvious. That she'd been made love to—deliciously ravished—by an alien being.

As the past few days were coming to a close she now admitted that her appetites had changed. Dramatically. Never a lover of tomatoes—juice, soup or otherwise—she was now craving them. Just the thought of her ordered Bloody Mary made her mouth water. Thinking of strawberries, cherries, or pomegranates sent her stomach to rumbling. Raw steak or hamburger would have been ambrosia.

All of these were red foods. Just as Az had predicted, she only seemed to crave the reddest dishes she could think of. The idea of eating anything that wasn't at least a little pink made her feel green around the gills. The image made her choke against a giggle as she remembered that Az was a water-dweller. She wondered if he had gills and then abruptly lost her mirth.

Her body was changing into something . . . *other*. It was more than evident through her conversations with Az and through her own observations. Having gills to go along with her bloody diet would not make her a happy camper.

Whatever Az was, whoever he was, he was real. And he'd claimed her for his own. What that meant for her in the future she couldn't guess. She was forced to admit that the only person who could answer her questions was the very man she was running from.

It all went back to Az. She would have to go back and hear him out. Give him a chance to explain everything and calm her fears.

"May I sit with you?" The deep voice broke over her reverie. It startled her.

Morrigan looked up . . . and up. When her eyes met the cloudy gray gaze of the tall man beside her she felt a moment of vertigo before she looked hastily away. Swallowing, she found her voice with some difficulty.

"It's a free country, isn't it?"

The man laughed. The sound echoed strangely in her ears. An eerie shiver ran down her spine.

"Of course it is. You're an American."

"Yes. Yes I am. You don't sound like you're from around here either, but I can't place your accent."

"I live in Greece presently, though I'm not from there originally." He smiled and offered her his hand with a practiced show of good cheer. "I'm Peter Smith."

Morrigan shook his hand. The contact of his skin against hers sent a jolt through her. It was a less than pleasant sensation. "Morrigan," she said, deliberately leaving off her last name. In her experience, far too many people remembered her name. It was difficult for her to just hand it out casually.

It didn't matter, he recognized her anyway.

"I greatly admire your work, Ms. Mederos." He sat upon the bench seat opposite her. When he didn't seem inclined to say more, she breathed a small sigh of relief. She couldn't handle a rabid fan just now.

"Thank you," she said, fleetingly wondering how she could escape his presence. His eyes did strange things to her. They were nearly unpleasant in their intense regard.

"You look tired, if you don't mind my saying so. Are you vacationing here or . . . "

"Yes, I'm on holiday," she lied easily.

She didn't know why, but she felt certain that she didn't want this man to know she was making her stay in Meigle a permanent one. Perhaps he was a reporter, she thought uneasily. That would explain her immediate dislike.

"It's a lovely town, full of history. But I'm sure that's why an artist like yourself would choose to come here. Not much to indulge along the lines of sightseeing and the like, though. The surrounding area is mostly just lochs and farmland."

"I like the lochs," she was moved to protest. "They're lovely."

"But of course you would think so," he said obscurely. She couldn't help but feel that he was making a joke at her expense.

The waitress deposited her drink on the table. She studied the dark ruby color of the liquid and was reminded of Az's blood. Her stomach growled, loud enough for the man to hear.

"Are you hungry? Let met buy you some food," he offered, as he waved for a waitress.

"No, that's all right. I'm not really that hungry," she protested.

"We both know that's not true, Morrigan. I can hear your stomach grumbling from over here. What would you like? I hear they have excellent stew here. Or perhaps you would prefer a light sandwich as it's so late?"

"No, thank you," she said hurriedly. "I'm just getting over a stomach flu and celebrating my return to health with my drink. I'm not in the mood to test the local fare just yet. I'll just grab some crackers when I get back to my . . . hotel."

"Where are you staying? Perhaps I could escort you there if you are feeling under the weather."

"No, that's all right. I think I'm going to go now." His gray eyes never wavered from hers and she felt an inexplicable urge to flee. He was making her nervous and jumpy, which was something she really didn't need at the moment.

"Thank you for your company," she said as she gathered her purse and made for the door.

"Until we meet again, Morrigan," she heard him mutter darkly as she fled the pub.

She certainly hoped that day never came. He was too creepy.

Seven

A SHORT WHILE later, Morrigan slowly opened the front door to her home. She felt like a teenager sneaking into her house after missing curfew, but she couldn't help herself. Tentatively, she laid her keys and purse on a table by the door and tiptoed into her den. She didn't know what she expected. She'd certainly never seen Az inside of her home outside of her dreaming mind, but she looked for signs of his presence anyway. With dramatic caution she went into each room, quietly searching for him.

He wasn't there.

She was almost disappointed but couldn't pinpoint why. Wasn't she supposed to be dreading this confrontation? Well . . . *wasn't* she? Her stomach growled as if in protest to her dark thoughts.

Morrigan padded softly into her bathroom where the candles she'd left burning had already flickered out. She drained the tub of its chilled water and cleaned up the mess on the floor. Grabbing a brush she went to work the tangles from her long tresses, gritting her teeth when the bristles snagged on the larger knots. Looking into the mirror she saw the deep shadows beneath her eyes. Her skin was paler than normal, translucent and fragile looking in the dim light of her room.

She winced and saw a brief flash of her teeth reflected back in the glass. Heart sinking, she raised unsteady hands to her lips and felt the ridge of her teeth beyond. Were her incisors longer? Yes, perhaps just a little bit. They certainly felt sharper, more pointed.

With a harsh gasp she jerked her hands away. She must be mistaken . . . she had to be. Her teeth were just fine, no sharper or longer than normal. If she wasn't careful she would soon imagine herself growing wings just like Az's.

With a nervous smile she rotated her shoulders. They seemed as normal as ever. "Just checking," she said aloud in a shaky voice.

For a moment longer she sat before the mirror, studying her reflection. Her thoughts were abuzz. Would it be so bad, after all, to quit worrying about the future and just see where it led? How did she feel about Az, her strange alien lover? Did she fear him or desire him or what?

"I love him," a tiny voice whispered from the depths of her soul.

How could she love him? She didn't even know what he was. Not really. Less than a few hours before she'd been terrified of him. Well, to be more honest, she had been terrified of what he was—what she was apparently turning into as well. Never in her life had she been more confused, or more at odds with her feelings.

What she did know was that she had felt joy and pleasure in his arms. Never before Az had she felt so cherished, so treasured. So loved. When he held her in his arms, or took her with his fangs and cock, she felt more alive than she ever had with any other lover.

The orgasms he gave her alone would make Az worth fighting for. She'd felt so alive in the tub as he'd pounded into her. When his hot cum had filled her sex she'd wanted to wring every possible drop he had to give and keep it there inside of her. She'd never wanted to let go. It was madness—it was irrational.

It was love.

All this time she'd run from him in her dreams, he'd never once threatened her with harm. He'd always seen to her pleasure, in every way, no matter how she'd screamed and cried at him. Every time she shied away from him in fear, he'd sought only to comfort her. He'd tried kissing away her cares, filling her with ecstasy. Tried to make her understand that she wasn't losing her mind.

No one had ever placed her welfare so highly above their own. And what had she done? She'd fled from him like a frightened child, undeserving of his love. Pushing him away with no regard for how he felt, she'd been too self-absorbed to see the gift that was being offered to her.

She had to find him.

Leaving her hair loose about her, she whirled from her bedroom and headed for the back door. With a sudden, desperate determination she decided she would look for Az in the only other place she knew to find him outside of her dreams. Her footfalls thudded dully against the ground as she made for the forest beyond her backyard.

Into the dark. Into the night.

Eight

THE DARK BLANKET of the night surrounded her. A light mist coated everything in sight, making it hard for her to see where she was going. She threw her hands out in front of her to keep the grasping branches from scratching her face and tangling in her hair.

Her eyes darted wildly about, searching the dark mist before her for some sign of the small clearing in which she'd met Az just the day before. Had it only been yesterday? It seemed like years had passed since then. She ran on and on through the forest, her breath leaving her lungs in harsh, sobbing gasps.

How much time passed she wasn't sure, but her side began to cramp. Her calves burned. She'd long since left behind the soft glow of the house lights and for a brief moment she feared that she was lost. But still she ran on, looking for Az.

Morrigan at last came upon the dark, smooth mirror of a small loch where she stumbled to a halt at the water's edge. She'd never seen this small body of water and knew she was hopelessly lost in the dark forest. Her running shoes grew wet as the water lapped at her toes, which quickly grew numb from the freezing water. It soaked and clung like black ink in the darkness.

With growing anticipation she stood there, staring. Her breasts trembled, rising and falling with her harsh, rapid pants. Her breath misted on the chill night air, wafting out in silver puffs from her quivering mouth. She sank to her knees by the pond, uncaring of the cold mud and water that quickly soaked through her jeans.

"Az, where are you?" Her voice echoed out across the water. "Az!"

There before her, a ripple broke the calm surface of the black pool of water. It was followed by another, and another. The water churned and lapped more forcefully against her knees from the force of the waves. Morrigan thought back to her earlier dreams of Az, when he'd emerged from the dark waters of a loch to stand before her.

"Az." Her heart shuddered within her breast.

Morrigan gasped and bit her lip as a dark head emerged from the heart of the loch. It was followed by Az's pale and heavily muscled form. He stepped over the water. His feet walked across its surface with barely a ripple as he passed. A small, mysterious smile played about his erotic lips. His black hair was dry and lay in soft waving curls down his back to his buttocks. He came to stand before her in all his masculine glory.

"At last you have come to me without coercion. I was beginning to think you never would," he said and took her hands in his. His skin was cool, as it always was when he first touched her.

"I'm not going to fight this anymore. I was wrong to be so cruel to you, but I was scared. I've never met anyone quite like you before." She gave a breathless laugh. "I've come to . . . I don't know. I just had to come and find you. I had to tell you th-that even though I don't really know how—no, that's not right." She waved her hands in agitation over her own ineloquence. "What I mean to say is that . . . I love you. I don't know how or why but I do. I really do."

His smile was blinding, and his fangs flashed in the moonlight. Two days ago the sight would have sent her screaming in terror, but now it only served to arouse her. He gave a full booming laugh. She jumped in surprise and then laughed along with him.

In a quick movement he gathered her up in his arms and swung her about in a circle. It would have been the most romantic moment of her life if she weren't so startled by the speed of it. He laughed once more and slowed. He stopped, still holding her with her feet dangling above the ground.

"I have searched for you for years, Morrigan. Never did I think I would actually find you, but my hope kept me going. I'm so glad it did. You've made me happy—truly happy. I promise to make you happy too."

He kissed her long and hard to seal the vow. She trembled against him, then he pulled back. "I am a cad. You hunger. I can feel your hunger beating at me through our bond."

"Y-yes. I *am* hungry," she admitted. Her lips trembled, and even as her stomach growled in proof, the words she spoke held more than just one meaning.

"Then let me sate your hunger." His voice was low and dark, enchanting her. Enslaving her. "Let me sate you in every way."

Nine

SHE LET LOOSE a breathy moan and leaned into his awaiting embrace. Az reached up with one hand, and a long, sharp talon appeared from the tip of one of his fingers. He drew the wicked looking nail in a long line across the thick muscle of his breast just above his nipple.

Blood welled from the wound, and his talon retracted back into the skin of his digit. Her eyes followed the path of a single drop of crimson as it trailed down his chest. Her stomach growled loudly in response to her awakened hunger.

"Drink from me, my mate. Be one with me at last." He reached out and pulled her head towards the wound.

It was so easy to cease her fight against the primal hunger that raged within her. She wondered why it had taken her so long. Then she fell upon him ravenously. His blood filled her mouth like a sweet and magical elixir, filling her with strength like she'd never before known.

She brought her hands up to his chest and lightly kneaded him with her nails. Mewling like a kitten, she drew deeply of his life-essence. On and on she suckled, satiating the deep hunger within her, until she felt replete at long last.

Drawing away from him she looked up with heavy lidded eyes. She knew her mouth was stained with his blood. She rose up to kiss him, smearing their lips with the wild, sweet taste of him. They kissed hungrily for several moments, stoking the fires between them.

Morrigan could feel the swell of his desire for her lying heavy and hot against her belly. She knew instinctively that he had fought and denied his release when she'd fed from him. Her lips trailed down his neck, lingering on his pulse, nipping gently at it with her teeth. She heard his swift intake of breath at her actions and smiled secretly to herself.

Moving lower she kissed and licked the already healing wound at his chest, drawing the last traces of blood away with her tongue and lips. Her teeth scraped gently at his nipple, and her tongue swirled around his areola to lave away the pain. She knew from the small moan that escaped his lips that he was enjoying her attentions. Eagerly, she gave the same treatment to his other nipple.

Licking a hot, wet path down his chest, Morrigan moved to kneel at his feet. The new position brought her face directly in front of his throbbing erection. Her hands roved over his stomach and thighs before moving to cup him between his legs. His heavy cock was powerful in her hands, raw and untamed.

Morrigan worshipped there at the altar of his powerful body. Her hands lovingly stroked along the great length and breadth of his cock. Knowingly, she paid special attention to the massive plum shaped head at its tip. A single glistening drop of glowing pre-cum glistened at the opening and she licked it away.

He tasted sugary, unlike any man she'd ever tasted before. She found herself ravenous for more. Leaning into him, she pressed a suckling kiss to the tip of his shaft. Her tongue darted out as she drew away to look up at him and wondered what he was thinking. What was he feeling?

Az groaned at the sight of her erotic hunger. He held her hair away from her face with one hand to better see her as she brought her face closer to him once more. He saw her glistening tongue dart out to lick from the base of his shaft to the tip. Then her lips opened wider to draw him deeply within the cave of her mouth. He felt the light scrape of her teeth against him and the swirling motions of her tongue as she suckled upon him. He'd never felt such overwhelming pleasure in all of his life.

This was his woman—his mate. He'd despaired of ever wooing her to his side willingly. She'd fought him so hard from the very beginning. No matter what had happened he would have waited for her, but his heart soared that his wait was over now. She was his.

He gave himself over to the pleasure of her mouth as she drew on him. The tip of his cock brushed the back of her throat and he groaned aloud. The muscles of her throat worked around him. Her tongue caressed his shaft like the heated brush of wet velvet. The pleasure was so intense that he couldn't help but move against her, fucking her mouth like he longed to fuck her tight cunt.

Morrigan's caressing hands felt his balls clench and draw up tightly against his body. She knew his climax was near and renewed her ministrations on his cock. Her head bobbed, moving faster and faster. She felt his fist tighten in her hair as he thrust into her mouth.

Never had she felt more powerful. His cock was heavy and hot in her mouth, the flesh smoother than satin. She sucked him for all she was worth, taking him so deeply into her throat she should have gagged. The head of his penis pulsed once inside her mouth, a second before his hot cum splashed against the back of her throat.

She gulped him down hungrily, savoring the sweet taste of his orgasm. Az let out a cry that reverberated throughout the forest. It thrilled her to her toes. He shuddered and thrust helplessly against her still suctioning mouth. She swallowed all he had to give and greedily sucked at the opening of his cock for more.

Az pulled reluctantly away from her and looked down at her swollen lips. A drop of his sperm glistened upon her lower lip, and he pushed it into her mouth with his forefinger, running the finger against her tongue as she lapped at it, savoring his unique flavor. His cock remained hard, hungry to find another release within her wet and welcoming cunt. He pulled her to her feet to stand before him.

"Remove your clothes, my beauty. I want you naked and ready for me. Whenever you are with me I want you to be naked."

More than eager for him to fulfill the sensual promise that was clearly written in his eyes, she rapidly shucked her clothing. When she stood in nothing but her black silk thong, Az prevented her from removing it.

"Gods, but I've never seen such a tantalizing sight," he muttered darkly before kneeling at her feet, much the same as she had done before him earlier.

Az lifted the strap of her thong away with his sharp teeth, licking and laving the soft curve of her hip as he tugged downward. He teased her through the silk with tiny nips, curving his seeking tongue beneath it. Morrigan gasped and dug her nails into the skin of his broad shoulders. He licked and bit at her sensitive flesh.

Moving down he sucked upon the swollen nub of her clit beneath the dark silk, and she arched against him with a strangled cry. He bared her, pulling her thong down away from her soaking femininity. He used his lips, teeth and tongue against her labia mercilessly.

At last she stood bare before him, her thong at her ankles. She stepped from the material, bringing her glistening copper curls closer to his face. He groaned and ran his hands up her thighs, making her knees grow weak with the erotic sensation of his touch. She was breathless with anticipation as he slowly lowered his head to her once more. His tongue darted out beyond the seam of his lips to delve into her heated core.

"I'll fall," she said on a moan. Her fingers dug into the flesh of his muscled shoulders.

"I'll catch you," he promised. His voice vibrated against her.

She pulled back slightly to watch as he parted her feminine folds with his fingers. He exposed her swollen and distended clit to the burning intensity of his gaze. The tips of his fingers grazed her pulsing nub of pleasure once, twice, half a dozen times. Morrigan squealed with the torturous pleasure of it and her knees gave out beneath her.

As he promised, Az caught her. His show of strength was immense as he lifted her before him and threw her legs about his shoulders. He buried his face between her legs. Hands supported her buttocks as he buried his face in her wet, pink flesh. His seeking tongue scraped against her clit over and over, bringing her closer and closer to peak.

As swollen as her clit was in her pleasure it was easy for him to suck her as thoroughly as she'd sucked him. Her clit disappeared into his mouth and his lips and tongue worked her until she was shrieking in ecstasy. A moment later she lost her last shred of self-control and she came in pulsing waves against his lips and tongue.

"Az," she cried out into the night. He made slurping sounds as he licked her wet, swollen flesh.

When the last waves of her orgasm had subsided, Az rose with her in his arms. Morrigan wrapped her legs around him and tried to impale herself upon his massive staff, desperate for the feel of his thick cock filling her. Az chuckled and held her seeking body away from its goal. He kissed her mouth fiercely, his lips still tasting faintly of her essence.

"Do not rush so, my mate. I will give you all that you desire in due time," he said in his enchanting voice.

"Fuck me, please," she begged shamelessly, tugging upon his silky hair in her frustration.

"I'll fuck you in just a moment if you'll be patient," he growled into her ear, clearly inflamed at her words.

Az set her down upon the forest floor with strong, steady hands. He turned her away from him and brought her hands up to rest against the trunk of an oak tree. Growling low in his throat, he came to stand close behind her. He used his feet to push at hers, spreading her legs wide.

His wide palm came to rest against the slight swell of her stomach, bringing her firmly against his burning hot cock. With one swift, harsh move he thrust into her wet pussy from his position behind her. She mewled and cried out, pushing more forcefully against him as he plunged balls deep into her.

"Do you want it hard and fast, or slow and deep?" he growled into her ear. His magical voice invaded her body in much the same way as his thickly aroused shaft.

"I don't care, I want it all," she cried desperately. Her breath was coming in harsh pants.

"Then I'll give it to you. All you can take, baby," he promised, before he withdrew from her clinging flesh.

Az withdrew from her until his erection was almost free of her. Then he thrust back into her with a force that flattened her buttocks against him and lifted her feet from the ground. She cried out with the pleasure that washed over her in drowning waves.

From his great height he leaned down and nipped at her shoulder. Then he laved the tiny hurt with his velvet tongue. Her hands dug into the bark of the tree and she thrust back to meet his pummeling cock. Their flesh made wet slapping sounds as he pounded her there against the tree.

The hand that was splayed upon her stomach moved downward to tangle in the curls between her legs, and his other hand came around to play at her nipples. He pulled upon her nipples and clit, overwhelming her with the pleasure of his expert caresses. Her pussy was stretched tight over his rod, burning deliciously with every deep thrust. She moaned and gasped aloud her pleasure, racing towards the edge of a glorious, shattering climax.

Suddenly, Az pulled away from her. Her cunt made a wet slurping sound as it greedily strove to keep his cock held prisoner. Az groaned harshly and turned her around to face him.

"I want you above me," he whispered into her mouth as he kissed her. "I want you to ride me. Hard. So I can see your breasts bounce and your face go slack with pleasure. I want to see your face when you come around my cock." He sucked her lip before drawing away to lie upon the forest floor.

"Won't you be uncomfortable?" she asked, concerned, even as her womb clenched with thrilling pleasure at his words.

"My wings will keep me cushioned," he said. Then his silver wings spread out beneath him.

The wings were so beautiful unfurled. At least twelve feet from tip to tip. They lay like gossamer silk beneath him. Morrigan had never seen such an erotic vision as Az splayed out upon the blanket of his iridescent wings. His cock was large and hard, bobbing and glistening in the moonlight, wet from her body. She fell upon him, dizzy with the force of her overwhelming hunger. Already starved for the pleasure of being in his arms.

Az's masterful hands guided her legs so that she came astride him, and she reached between them to position his penis. She sank down upon him with a breathy moan. Her wet flesh swallowed him deep within her. They could both feel her flesh pulse around him and he dug his fingers into the flesh of her bottom. He was visibly fighting against losing control.

He threw his head back slightly and his glowing eyes were dazed. His mouth parted to reveal long, sharp incisors. She fell upon him to press her lips against his teeth. It sent his cock impossibly deeper into her.

They kissed and Az guided her movements upon him with hands at her bottom. He moved her over his cock, thrusting his hips with each undulation of her hips against him. His teeth pulled and bit at her lips, drawing a faint trace of blood with his impassioned kisses. He laved the small hurt he inflicted, but she loved the pleasure-pain and pressed her lips harder against his teeth. Both of their mouths were filled with the coppery tang of her blood.

Her wild response sent him over the edge of his control. His body pounded fiercely into her, faster and faster. He pulled her forcefully against him as he moved within her, grinding against her clit with every down thrust. Morrigan's orgasm washed over her, twisting her body upon a rack of unimaginable pleasure. Her vagina tightened around his pummeling flesh, milking him with her pulsating muscles until he too found release. He pumped his hot cum into her depths, roaring his satisfaction into the night.

Morrigan collapsed upon him, witless and gasping. Az's hands came up to tenderly cradle her head for his kiss before they rested limply upon her back. He was unable to move but for his harsh breathing and pounding heart.

"I've never felt so much pleasure in all my life," he praised her. His voice was deep and ragged.

"Me neither," she confessed shakily against his chest. She burrowed against him like a kitten, breathing deep of his deliciously masculine scent.

"We were made for this—for one another," he stated.

"I believe you," she said, knowing his words were true and heartfelt. She agreed with him. She felt so right in his embrace. She knew it couldn't have been any other way. Her heart swelled with emotion and she kissed his chest, resting her face against him.

They lay there quietly on the forest floor for several moments. Az's wings came around to enfold her more tightly against him. The silky wings protected her exposed skin from the chill night air, keeping her safe and close to him.

Morrigan sighed with contentment, feeling truly at peace for the first time in she couldn't remember how long. With her core still wet and pulsing, and Az's shaft still buried deeply within her, she let her eyes grow heavy. She relaxed fully against him and fell into a light doze.

Ten

"WELL, WELL, WELL. What do we have here? A horny Icari and his human slut." The masculine voice broke over their contentment.

Az tensed beneath Morrigan, his wings enfolding her even more tightly against him. His amethyst eyes blazed angrily. "I know that voice," Az called out darkly, as he made to rise. Morrigan was still held protectively in his arms as he gained his feet.

"Indeed? I was almost certain you would have forgotten your old childhood friend by now, Azure," the disembodied voice called from the darkness.

"Show yourself Petiyr," Az demanded in a regal tone that brooked no argument.

The tall, dark figure of a man emerged from the thicket of trees directly before them. Morrigan gasped as a shaft of silver moonlight illuminated the features of a familiar face.

"Peter Smith?" she asked in confusion.

"No my dear, the name is Petiyr. Please do get it right now that you've heard it pronounced correctly."

"Peter, Petiyr, who gives a flying rat's ass how you pronounce it? What I want to know is why the hell you are even here?"

"I followed you of course, my foolish little human. I knew you'd lied to me about staying in a hotel and I wanted to know why. You didn't go back to a hotel, but to a house. *Your* house. And even though you seem to be enjoying a bit of recreational activity here with our winged friend, I don't think you're merely vacationing either."

Az tightened his hold upon her. "How do you know this man, Morrigan?"

"We met in a pub earlier this evening. He was looking at me strangely and offered to buy me dinner. He made me uncomfortable so I left. I didn't know he would follow me."

"Yes, well, perhaps I was a bit worried about you. But then again, perhaps not. You looked a little peaked tonight, Morrigan. Your skin was pale, and I could clearly see that your gums were drawing away from your incisors. It was a look I had seen before. One I'm very familiar with. In addition, I also smelled the cum of our rutting friend here, pooled between your lovely thighs." He laughed maniacally when her cheeks flushed with mortification.

"I thought you were banished to the far reaches of Icaria, for your perfidy against the women of our homeworld. How came you to be here, Petiyr?" The words coming from Az's mouth sounded so formal and regal that Morrigan couldn't help but stare dumbstruck from one man to the other.

"Ahh, yes. Your brother, the King, *did* banish me from the Azrine court for my ravishment of the fair Ilyana. Without a fair trial, I might add. How could he have taken the word of the city's most infamous whore over the word of his little brother's best friend? She was asking for my attentions—begging for them. I merely gave her what she so desperately wanted."

"You brutalized her. You negated all bonds of friendship between us with your cruel actions. Our males are bound by law to protect all females, be they family, friend or stranger. We are too strong to visit violence upon their delicate forms. Yet you disobeyed our most sacred law by raping and beating Ilyana. You deserved your punishment."

Petiyr's gray eyes blazed, though not near as brightly or ethereally as Az's. Morrigan struggled to follow their conversation.

"You're an Icari, too?" she asked, puzzled.

Petiyr flashed her a grin from behind tightly clenched teeth. "That I am, Morrigan."

"But where are your wings? Where are your fangs? And your eyes have pupils and visible whites, but Az's don't. You don't look anything like him."

"Well, aren't we just full of observations? My wings were cut off as part of the punishment when I was banished from our fair Azrine. It was done to prevent me from swimming back too easily, and to keep me from leaving our homeworld.

"But I didn't much care for my exile on the desert plains of Navbeth. I snuck back towards civilization, abducting the first winged Icari that crossed my path. It was easy. I forced him to take me here, to this gods-forsaken planet. I had been here, once before, with Azure when he'd left on the quest to search for his mate many years ago. I remembered how weak and frail the people here were compared to my kind, and decided I would like being one of the strongest, fastest beings on the planet. Upon our arrival, I killed my transport and disposed of his body. "

Morrigan tried not to react to the cold dead tone of Petiyr's voice as he spoke so casually of killing someone. She burrowed back against the firm wall of Az's chest, gaining comfort in his strength.

"But what about your teeth and your eyes? I've never known an

Icari to look so . . . wasted away." Az's beautiful voice broke the small silence.

"When I first arrived here, everything was fine. Peachy keen, as Morrigan might say." He flashed her an evil grin, and she fought not to cringe away from the disturbing sight. "I drank the blood of these weak humans, and used my charms to seduce hundreds of women. I grew rich off of the spoils of those whom I killed.

"I was careful not to alarm too many people. This planet is notorious for stamping out the existence of beings such as I without a second thought. No matter how strong I was, I would have been no match against a large show of force should I be discovered. So I lived quietly, taking what I wanted from whomever I wanted. It was a perfect existence for me. I was happy as I had never been.

"But years passed. Ten long years. My body started to change. It seems, old friend, that the atmosphere of this planet is not entirely friendly to our kind with prolonged exposure. My fangs receded into my gum line, and I could not draw them forth—even with pliers, which I foolishly used in my desperation. The glowing brilliance of my eyes faded until they looked more human than Icari. I regressed into something less than an Icari, losing some of my good looks and preternatural senses. I have grown to hate my new prison as much as I hated my old one."

"And your strength? Are you still strong enough to match me, Petiyr?"

"You couldn't let that question lie unspoken between us, could you Az? I could lie and say that I am still as strong as ever I was, but I will not waste my breath. I could not face you in a fair test of strength. This accursed planet has seen to that."

Az moved to set Morrigan behind him, and started forward, but Petiyr stopped him with a laugh. Petiyr's hand moved and the moonlight glinted upon the barrel of the gun he held.

"Don't be foolish, Az. I am not totally unprepared to face you, as you can see."

"What do you want with us, Outcast?"

"Well, I'll probably fuck this little bitch here before I kill her. Then you can take me back to Icari, and the Azrine court. With you as my hostage, Azure, I'm sure to gain a pardon from your brother, and I will at last be back where I belong."

Morrigan put her hands against Az's wings, applying pressure when he made to move towards Petiyr. His anger washed over her in waves. It was a physically palpable thing on the chill night air. But he didn't stand a chance against a gun no matter how angry he was. She couldn't bear the thought of Petiyr hurting Az.

She probably should have been more concerned for her own welfare, especially after hearing Petiyr's plans for her. But she could only think about Az's safety. She loved him, more than her own life. She didn't care what happened to her.

Even though she only knew him through her dreams and recently with her body, she knew instinctively that they were perfect for each other. Knew that they belonged to one another down to their very souls. She loved him and she would do all that she could to keep him safe.

Even at the risk of her own life.

Eleven

"LET MORRIGAN GO free, unharmed, and I will do as you ask," Az grated out.

"No, I don't think so, Az. You are not properly cowed yet. There's no telling what you might do when I am at your mercy in the pools between our worlds. I will fuck her, kill her, and you will get to watch. If she is indeed your mate, as her physical changes do seem to attest, then you will weaken with her death. You will be totally in my power, and therefore less of a threat on our journey."

"I will never be weak enough for you to control. If you harm her then I will simply refuse to aid you. If you let her go, I will take you safely back to Icari. I give you my word of honor."

Petiyr snorted. "I don't care about your professed honor. I don't trust it."

"That is simply because you have no honor, Petiyr. I have never broken my word once it is given, this you know. Let her go, and I will do as you wish."

There was a long moment of silence as the two men faced each other.

"No. I'm not leaving without a nice piece of ass to tide me over," Petiyr said before he rushed him.

Unprepared for the attack, Az fell to the ground, dazed under the cruel blow of Petiyr's gun against his temple. Petiyr turned and fell upon Morrigan, his long tongue rasping out to lick a rough line down her cheek. They both tripped and fell to the ground.

"You're a total, fucking lunatic," Morrigan yelled, struggling against him.

Petiyr laughed maniacally, his eyes wild as his hands fell upon her exposed breasts with bruising force. His gun flew from his hand when her arm met his wrist with a jarring blow, but he didn't seem to care. He tried to insinuate himself between her thighs, but her legs were kicking too violently to allow it.

"Fight me, baby. I love it when whores like you put up a fight. It makes your subjugation so much sweeter."

Morrigan gagged when he tried to kiss her. Then she managed to bite down upon his lips, tearing flesh and drawing blood. The taste of his blood was sour and coppery—nothing like Az's. She spat it back at him when it filled her mouth. Petiyr cried out and pulled back. She scrambled away from him, crawling crablike on her hands and feet backwards into the darkness.

"You bitch! You'll pay for that," he roared, coming forward over her once more. He rose back to hit her with his clenched fist.

Morrigan's hand closed over the handle of Petiyr's fallen gun. With grateful surprise, she grasped at it with desperate fingers. She wasn't quite quick enough and his fist fell against her cheekbone, making her see stars. Her vision dimmed and swam as Petiyr fell upon her with renewed violence.

As her attacker fell between her legs, his hand moving to the fastening of his trousers, she recovered slightly from his vicious blow. Her fingers tightened upon her weapon and she swung up to level it at his face.

"Back off, asshole," she said in a voice that sounded diamond hard, even to her own still ringing ears.

"What the fuck?" Petiyr choked in disbelief as he stared cross-eyed down the barrel of his own gun.

"Yeah, that's right. Your would-be victim—little ol' me—has found your gun. And oh—guess what! I know how to use it, too," she said as she released the gun's safety catch with her thumb.

She shoved the weapon ruthlessly into his face, butting it against his nose with bruising force. "Now back off, psycho, or I'll pull this trigger."

Petiyr backed off of her slowly. "You couldn't kill me," he scoffed. "You don't have what it takes to end a life."

"I've just spent several years of my life learning to protect myself from rabid fans and stalkers. I can assure you that after all that time I'm completely fucking ready to shoot your ass. Do you really want to try me?"

Apparently he didn't because he continued to back away from her, until she had enough room to move away and gain her feet. She looked down at him with hard eyes, the gun held steadily at his face. Her eyes never strayed from him as she went to check on Az.

Az's powerful body stirred when she approached him, and she spared a quick glance at him. Obviously he was a little dazed, and a dark trickle of blood marred his temple and cheek. Beyond that he looked as gorgeous as always.

"Are you all right?" she asked, careful to keep the gun trained upon Petiyr, who was crouched upon the ground.

Az chuckled as he dizzily gained his feet. He came beside her and saw the surly, huddled figure of Petiyr as Morrigan held the gun pointed at him. He shook his head and pressed a fleeting kiss against her cheek.

"I never thought you would be the one to save me, my love," he said.

"Never underestimate a woman with a firearm. We're not all marshmallows and sunshine—we've got a dark side a mile wide."

Az laughed loudly into the night. Morrigan couldn't resist smiling at the sound of his good cheer.

"Gods, you both make me sick," Petiyr grumbled. His lips curved in an ugly sneer.

"As for you, Petiyr. You, I will take back to Icari to be tried for your crimes against our people and the people of Earth. Though we haven't sentenced death to anyone in centuries, I am sure that my brother will see fit to make an exception for you. You are a disgrace to our people, Petiyr. You deserve the ultimate punishment of death."

Az's words appeared to enrage Petiyr anew and he seemed to lose what was left of his self-control. He rushed at Az once again, but this time Az was prepared. In a lightning quick move, before Morrigan even had a chance to pull the trigger of her gun, Az had cuffed Petiyr upon the head with enough force to knock him out cold. Morrigan hadn't even seen him move.

"*Good grief,*" she choked out, staring at Az with wide eyes. Aside from the blood at his temple he didn't looked fazed at all by his stunning display of speed and strength.

"Are you all right, my love?" His eyes tenderly roved over her, reminding her that she was still completely naked.

"I'm fine, just a little bruised is all," she said breathlessly under his roving eyes. Unbelievably she felt her desire for him stir anew, despite the odd situation in which they found themselves. She wondered if it would always be this way between them.

"Your face will bruise. Your breasts too, where he hit you. I am sorry I was too weak to help you, Morrigan." His eyes were dim with shame.

Morrigan smiled impishly and lowered the gun as he approached her. "Don't be sorry. It wasn't your fault that he didn't fight fair. Besides, I'm a twenty-first century woman. I know how to take care of psycho males with guns," she laughingly said.

"Oh really? And can you take care of *me*?" he asked with a wicked smile. He slipped his arms around her waist, bringing her body into full contact with his own. His staff was already hard and heavy. She couldn't help but respond by wriggling against him erotically, cuddling his erection.

Az drew away from her with a serious look in his eyes.

"Will you think about coming with me back to my home world? I have to leave without you for now. I have to take Petiyr before the court to face my brother's justice. But I'll be back in a few short days to talk about it with you if you want."

Morrigan thought about it. A new world! The idea was thrilling, even as it was terrifying. "I don't have any family here, or friends that I would miss if I were to leave," she said, warming up to the idea of it. Then another thought intruded. "But wait. How can I go with you? I can't exactly breathe underwater, you know."

Eyes serious, he looked over her closely. "You're already changing, my love. In time you'll grow to be more like me, and breathing underwater will be the first of those changes. Or so I'm told. We'll wait as long as necessary for your body to adapt itself before we go to Icaria. Time is of no importance to us now, with your increased longevity."

"What do you mean by increased longevity? Wait a minute, just how old *are* you, Az?"

"I'm only one hundred and twelve. I am still a young man

among my people. You and I have many Earth lifetimes yet to be together."

"Good grief! This will take some getting used to. Are you sure you would want to have me around for that long?"

"You are my mate, destined to be at my side through our life and beyond. I could not live my life without you. I love you."

Morrigan's eyes filled tears. "Oh Az, I love you, too. I don't know how or why, but I do. More than I've ever loved anyone or anything. Of course I'll go with you to Icaria." She buried her face in his neck as he held her tightly to him.

Morrigan was the first to pull away. "Now you'd better go and get psycho-boy here back to your brother, the king. King! Does that make you a prince, Az?" She couldn't keep the apprehension from her voice. She'd already left one high-profile life behind her. She certainly didn't relish embarking upon another.

"Indeed it does, though it is merely an empty title. There's no real power behind it. Does that displease you, my love?"

"Good God, no," she laughed, relieved. "I've had enough of fame and glory to last me several lifetimes, thank you. I'm ready to settle down in quiet anonymity for the rest of my days, and that's no lie."

Petiyr chose that moment to groan, and he stirred on the ground at their feet. Az sighed. "I'd better see to him now. Will you be here waiting for me, Morrigan, when I return?"

"I'll wait as long as it takes," she promised.

She didn't have very long to wait. Three days later, her love returned to her, and together they entered the waters that would take them to their home.

Dream On

JACI BURTON

To Briana St. James, my wonderful editor.
Thank you for helping me realize a lifelong dream.

To Charlie, the man of my dreams. You are my heart and my very soul. Without you, I would be forever lost. With you, I am whole. Thank you for making me believe that anything I dream can come true. I love you.

"We are such stuff
As dreams are made on . . . "
William Shakespeare's *The Tempest* (IV, i, 156–157)

One

KATE STOOD OUTSIDE on the porch and wrapped the quilt around her shoulders to ward off the chill of impending night. Dust filtered through the setting sun, coloring the lake a rusty orange. It was spring and the days were beginning to grow warmer, but at night when the sun went down so did the temperature. She shivered, grabbed her cup of tea and sat on the old wooden swing. As she rocked back and forth and watched the orange glow of the horizon, the memories slapped at her like flies at a summer picnic.

Spring used to be Jack's favorite time of year. During the rare occasions he had a weekend to spare, they'd travel out here to the country house and sit on the swing, talking about anything and everything. His job, the kids, what they wanted to do when they retired. They'd made so many plans together, counting the years until the kids were grown and off creating their own lives.

The kids were gone now. Problem was, so was Jack. Only his departure had been more abrupt. One day he was there, sharing his life with her, and the next he was gone. Without any warning, he'd disappeared from her life completely.

Her mellow mood vanished in an instant, replaced instead by the cool chill that had permeated every day for the last five years. And all because of Jack.

The sonofabitch. She'd go to her grave hating him for what he'd done.

He'd made promises. Big promises about their future together, sucking her into his dreams so easily, only to shatter her illusions in one day. Now she was forty-five years old and alone, and all those things Jack had promised her for twenty years had meant nothing. They'd never enjoy making love in the middle of the day because the boys were no longer there to interrupt. They'd never sell their house in the city and retire here in their country house. They'd never grow old together.

Empty words. Betrayal.

"You lied to me, Jack," she whispered to the breeze swirling around her. "You promised me forever and you didn't keep your part of the bargain. How could you do this to me? How could you make promises and not keep them?"

Swiping at the tears rolling down her cheeks, she summoned up the righteous anger that always made her feel better. Screw him! He'd left her after twenty years, destroying her dreams. She'd long ago vowed never to hurt over him again. Better to stay angry. Much more productive that way.

So why did she still dream about him at night? Why did his face, his touch, still haunt her?

Because you can't let go.

She shook her head, refusing to dwell on him any longer. Jack was part of her past now and the house in the city was up for sale. One part of her memories would soon be gone. At least she still had the country house, even though it was way too quiet these days with the boys gone. Both Ron and J.J. were in college, but they came home as often as they could.

They worried about her, and she knew that. They tried to visit as often as possible and she knew it was because they were concerned about the amount of time she spent alone. But she fought them tooth and nail, insisting they make their own lives. The last thing she needed or wanted was her children acting as babysitters.

She was fine alone. She'd even reached the point where she could spend weekends here at the country house like they all used to. Soon she'd live here full-time and could concentrate more on her writing. Being alone would be advantageous then. She could write undisturbed by city noise. Maybe she'd even be able to crank out one extra book a year this way. And occasionally, the boys could visit since the country house was closer to their school. They were supposed to be there this weekend, but she insisted they stay at school for the big game. Besides, the quiet solitude of the country would be good for her muse. Maybe she'd be able to finish that book this weekend.

She stood and headed into the house, locking the door and flipping the light switches off. She undressed and stood in front of the bathroom mirror, shaking her head at how much she'd aged in the past five years. Her face drooped like a basset hound's, her hair hung long and stringy and the once shiny auburn strands looked oily and dirty. She'd gained at least fifteen pounds and felt every single one of them in her belly, thighs and butt.

"What the hell do I have to look good for, anyway?" she mused to her reflection. "I used to take care of myself, worked hard on my body and my appearance. Did it keep Jack in my life?"

The reflection shook its head.

"Exactly my point. No one sees me anyway." And her sons loved her no matter how she looked, though they did suggest she get out more and away from her computer.

What they really meant was they thought she should find another man.

The thought of dating anyone made her shudder in revulsion. Never again would she put her trust in a man, only to have her dreams of paradise ripped away when he didn't live up to his promises.

She grabbed her pajamas and slipped them on, remembering the days she and Jack would slide under the cool sheets stark naked, using their bodies to warm each other. With a sigh she shut off the light and climbed into bed, staring out the window at the half moon shining overhead.

They used to make love while looking out this window. The moon always had an erotic pull for her, reminding her of hot and sexy whispered promises in the dark, warm, calloused hands reaching for her breasts or between her legs, eliciting cries in the night that she hadn't experienced in far too long.

Her breasts ached and a tightness formed between her legs. Her clit throbbed, her pussy moistening at the memories of hot sex that went on all night long. She reached down, sliding her hand between her legs and resting the heel of her palm against her clit. Pleasure burst inside her, but she quickly drew her hand away, refusing to give in to the desire that seemed all too insistent these days. Orgasm would only make her wish for something she couldn't have.

Sexual reawakening wasn't what she needed right now. She'd long ago lost the urge to bring herself to orgasm, afraid the memories would wash over her and she'd end up hating Jack, and herself, for what they could have had together. So she fought back the urges, determined that her mind was stronger than her body and she didn't need sex of any kind to feel fulfilled.

Disgusted by her unruly body, she flipped over onto her back and stared up at the ceiling. "Damn you, Jack, will I ever get over what you did?"

Maybe the boys were right and she should get out and start dating again. If she did, thoughts of Jack would dwindle until there was nothing left but vague memories. But could she really do that? Thoughts of having another man's hands on her or another man seeing her naked made her physically ill. Jack was the only one who'd ever touched her, the only one she'd ever wanted to touch her.

Could she actually take that step and start over again? She let the thought permeate her mind for a few minutes, but came up with no answers to her dilemma other than the same old feeling that she belonged to Jack and nobody else. That she'd never let another man touch her.

But was that fair? Why did she have to be punished because of what Jack did?

"Somebody please tell me what to do." She laid there quietly for a few moments, but the darkness provided no answer. Not that she expected one. No one had answers or explanations for why Jack had left her. Only the standard diatribes of *these things happen* and *no one can explain why*, or *give it time and you'll get over him*, and of course her favorite one of all . . .

. . . *it's not your fault.*

With a disgusted sigh, she squeezed her eyes shut and refused to think anymore tonight.

Sleep, Kate. Turn your mind off. Maybe one day you'll actually be able to get through an entire day and not think about that bastard who left you.

Maybe one night she could sleep without the dreams haunting her.

If only . . .

"Kate? Wake up."

Kate pulled the covers over her shoulders and turned away from the offending voice. "Go away. I'm sleeping."

Warm breath caressed her neck and goose bumps broke out on her skin when a hand touched her shoulder.

"Babe, you need to wake up."

So used to him invading her dreams every night, she ignored the realistic sound of his voice. Why wouldn't he just go away? How long would this torment continue? "Get lost, Jack."

"I've *been* lost, Katie. I'm home now."

Something wasn't right. This conversation didn't *feel* dream-like. It felt real.

But that wasn't possible. Jack didn't live here anymore. He wouldn't be here. No way. She was hallucinating, or so deep into the dream that it seemed like the real thing. Yet she'd dreamed of him every single night since he left and this wasn't like all those times before. Her nightly sojourns had been more surreal, more distant. Though she saw him, touched him, made love with him over and over again, there was a definite lack of reality to her dreams. It was if she was observing her own body, watching the way he touched her and kissed her.

This was different. The covers moved down and she felt the chill of cold air on her skin. When the brush of warm fingers trailed down her arm, she knew what she felt was no dream.

Her heart lurched and she sat up, blinking back the sleep from her eyes. The room was dark, but she heard the soft inhalation of breath that wasn't her own. She broke out into a sweat and fought to still the trembling of her body.

Someone was in the room with her!

Too afraid to even swallow, she clutched the sheets and prayed to God one of her kids had come home for the weekend to surprise her.

"Don't be afraid, Kate. It's me."

She blinked, as if the act of doing so would cast a light over whoever was in the room.

"Baby, shhh, it's okay."

That voice. She knew that voice. But it couldn't be. It wasn't possible. When he left she knew he was never coming back. And he hadn't in five long years.

It couldn't be him.

She lifted her arm, ready to search the darkness, but dropped her hand to the sheets and shook her head, realizing that she'd completely lost her mind. "You're not real." This was the weirdest dream she'd ever had.

But when a calloused hand caressed her cheek, she froze. Dammit, she *felt* that! It *was* real! She wasn't asleep now, so it had to be real. Surely she wasn't still dreaming.

"Don't be afraid."

Her eyes adjusted well enough to the darkness to make out a silhouette of a man sitting on the edge of her bed. "Who the hell are you?"

It's not Jack. It couldn't be him. He would never come back. Yet the more she cast it aside, the more real it became.

"You know damn well who I am. Wake up, Kate. This isn't a dream."

It *had* to be a dream. No way in hell would Jack have come back to her. Not after . . .

This was ludicrous. And it wasn't happening. If she reached for him, she'd grasp nothing but air. Lifting her hand, she stretched toward the apparition in the darkness and grabbed a fistful of . . .

. . . shirt. Shirt surrounding hard muscle of a man's upper arm.

Oh, God. This wasn't happening. Jerking her hand away, she scooted toward the other edge of the bed and lunged for the lamp on her nightstand, afraid to turn the light on and too afraid not to. She sucked in a breath of courage and flicked the switch.

Holding her breath, she turned around. Her heart tumbled over as she drank her fill of the man she both loved with all her heart and hated to the deepest recesses of her soul.

"Jack."

Two

IT COULDN'T BE. He wouldn't be here. How would he even know she was here? Why would he even *want* to find her? Not a word in five years. Nothing. No contact.

Why now?

"I can explain," he said, running his hand through his thick black hair. "If you want to hear it."

He hadn't changed at all in five years. She had aged like an old hag and blamed stress and misery as the reasons her appearance had changed so drastically. Apparently he'd not had that problem. His body was still all corded muscle, expansive chest, flat abs and sexy, muscular thighs encased in jeans that hugged his form like a second skin. She pulled the covers up to her chin, suddenly wishing she'd never turned that light on.

How dare he look so goddamned sexy!

Drawing up the anger she lived with every day, she lifted her chin and said, "No explanations necessary. You left. There's nothing else to say. Get out."

He stood and walked around the other side of the bed to sit next to her. She tried to scoot away but he grasped her wrist. Heat surged through her body at his touch. She might hate him, but just the whisper of his skin against hers flamed her long-dead libido to life again.

"I have a lot to say. And I left for a good reason."

She snorted. "Sure you did. There's always a good reason to dump a twenty-year marriage just like that." Okay, she sounded like a shrew. A bitter one at that. But she didn't care. She'd spent five years wishing she could get him alone in a room and tell him exactly what she thought of him. Now was her chance. And no matter what her heart said, no matter the joy that wanted to spring up inside her at the sight of him, she held onto her anger like a comforting weapon to use against him.

"I never stopped loving you, Katie."

Oh, now that wasn't fair. Wasn't fair at all. She'd been prepared for excuses, for apologies and explanations, but not this.

Pull that anger and feeling of betrayal out of their shell, Katherine. Tell him how it felt when you woke up one morning and he was gone.

"You never loved me. Hell, you barely even told me you loved me the last few years before you left." *And if you really loved me, you'd never have left me.*

Furrows creased his brow. She itched to trace every single line on his face, all the way down to the curve of his full lips. His gray eyes darkened like a thick cover of clouds in the night and he dropped his chin, looking at her through hooded eyes. "I'm sorry. You're right. There's a lot I have to atone for, if you'll let me."

She jumped out of bed and paced the room, brushing her hair away from her face, no longer caring that he could see her gray hair and flabby body. "Atone? Atone! How *dare* you show up here claiming 'Gee babe, I'm sorry that I left you five years ago, but I'm back now so everything's okay, right?'. How stupid do you think I am? Do you think I've sat around for five years mourning what we had, missing you so bad I couldn't breathe and just wishing I had one more day with you?"

He didn't smile, but he nodded. "Actually, I think you did just that. And that's exactly how I felt, too. That's why I'm back."

Damn. Fury rocked her body and she trembled. She dropped into the chair next to the desk and bent her head down, refusing to let her ire completely overtake her. She clasped her hands tightly together to still the tremors. He wouldn't hurt her again. She'd never allow it. Once was bad enough. Twice would be unbearable.

"Why are you here? What do you want from me?"

He didn't answer and she refused to look up at him. But she heard him move off the bed and toward her. She couldn't help but watch as he knelt on the floor in front of her. She squeezed her eyes shut so she didn't have to look at him, afraid if she did she'd weaken, and all those years spent erecting the protective shell around her heart would have been wasted.

"Katie, I love you. And I made some serious mistakes with our marriage. I screwed up our lives and our future together. But I didn't leave because I didn't love you anymore. I left because I had to, because I had no control over certain events. It wasn't until after I'd left that I realized there were things I needed to fix about myself."

"And did you?"

"Did I what?"

105

"Did you fix them?"

"I don't know. I hope so. Actually, I thought you could tell me, if you give me a chance to show you."

His words filtered through her anger like honey into a comb. Her shell weakened at the husky plea in his voice and she remembered all those whispered promises in the dark, when his hard, thick cock had filled her, his hands stroking her to one whimpering orgasm after another. He'd played her body like an artist inspired to greatness, each brush of his hands and mouth on her like a masterpiece of rapture that made her cry out and beg for more of his genius.

The bad times had been all too frequent, but the good times were incredibly memorable.

"Let me prove it to you, Katie. Tell me what you want."

How easy it would be to tell him to stay, to let him know that all she'd ever wanted was forever with the man she loved. But the last five years wouldn't disappear so easily, even if her body was starved for attention and her heart felt empty and cold without him. She looked him in the eye, making sure he read every one of her emotions. "What I want is for the last five years to have never happened. What I want is for the five years before that to have been more than fleeting glimpses of you while you stopped at home to unpack and repack in between business trips. What I want is to start over again and this time have a husband who'd be there for me and the kids instead of focused only on his career."

She refused to feel sympathy for the pain in his eyes. None of this was her fault.

"You're right. About everything. I screwed up. But I can't go back. I can only go forward. Let me show you that I've changed. Let me give you back what I took from you when I left."

"You can never give me back what I've lost, Jack. Never." And she didn't care how much she hurt him by saying it. It was the truth.

Besides, she'd had this conversation with him almost every night for the past five years, when he appeared in her dreams. This time seemed real, but she knew better. She was still dreaming. She had to be.

She jerked when he swept his hand over her hair.

"Let me try."

She pushed at him and stood, crossing over to the sliding glass doors and looking out at the moon. "I don't want anything. I don't want you here." She turned fully away when he stepped behind her, determined not to let him touch her again. "You showing up out of the blue like this after no word for five years is ripping my heart out, Jack. Please leave me alone. I was doing fine without you."

Because despite her anger, her misery, her desperate prayers to bring him back and then giving up when she knew her pleas fell on deaf ears, she'd never once stopped loving him. Standing here with him now opened up wounds that had taken years to close. This wasn't fair!

"I'm not leaving this time, Katie, no matter what you say. I'm here to stay, for as long as it takes to show you I've changed. I'm staying until you realize that I love you, that I've always loved you and I never stopped."

Then why did you leave me?! The words dangled on the tip of her tongue, but she refused to give them voice. What difference would explanations make at this point?

"Just go away, Jack. I don't want or need you anymore." She pushed past him and went into the bathroom and shut the door. She sat on the lid of the toilet and counted, hoping he'd get the hint and leave.

Twenty minutes later her butt was numb. Was he gone or had he stayed? It was quiet and he'd long ago stopped talking to her through the door, so maybe he'd finally given up and left. She unlocked the door and opened it, both relieved and disappointed that she didn't find him waiting for her in her bedroom.

Oh, sure. Just like that, in and out of her life once again. She tasted the bitterness, reveled in it, wrapped it around her like a shield of thick armor. Anger felt so much better than pain. It strengthened rather than weakened her, filling her with its lusty power like a weapon she could use against her enemies.

Or enemy. The man she once loved had become her nemesis. Only this time she wasn't going to come out the loser. She didn't need him in her life again, didn't love him anymore and he wasn't welcome in her home.

Giving up on getting anymore sleep, she glanced at the clock.

Five in the morning. Might as well fix some coffee, clear her head and try to get some writing done. Sleep would come later, after she thoroughly exhausted herself.

She padded into the kitchen, stopping in the hallway as she picked up the scent of coffee. Wary, she peeked around the corner, her shoulders slumping in defeat as she spied Jack leaning against the counter, a cup of steaming coffee in one hand, holding another out to her with the other.

"How about some breakfast, babe? I'll cook."

Oh, God. She wanted to fall into a heap right there in the doorway, pound her head against the wood floor and scream out in rage, letting all the emotions she'd held in pour out of her. She wanted, no, *needed* an epic tantrum.

Why was he doing this to her?

Three

KATE REGARDED JACK with a dubious expression. Okay, if this is the way he was going to play the game, so be it. She'd let him know that she had changed in the five years he'd been gone. That she was self-sufficient and didn't really need him anymore. That she was impervious to his dark good looks, his steely body, his sexy smile and voice.

Yeah, right. Now she just had to convince herself of it.

True to his word, he fixed her breakfast. Didn't let her do a thing except sit at the table, forcing her to watch the way he moved, the way his ass looked when he bent over to retrieve a pan from the lower cabinet, the way his muscles moved under his tight T-shirt.

Even with bacon sizzling in the pan, the scent of Jack overpowered her. Crisp, clean, smelling like his favorite soap. She'd left his brand of soap in the shower long after he'd left, torturing herself by lifting it off the shelf and inhaling the smell that was so much a part of him it made her heart hurt.

Smelling it again and seeing him standing in their kitchen cooking for her made her hands shake. Fighting off the quiver in her fingers, she lifted the coffee cup to her lips and took a deep draw of the life-infusing caffeine, hoping it would jolt her out of the cloud of bittersweet memories.

Remember the bad stuff, Kate.

Bad stuff. Right. That she could do. Like a life preserver, she held tight to those memories. Jack had been all about work. Owning his own business was time-consuming, he'd told her in the beginning. And it eventually consumed all of him. He never took the time to do the things she wanted. But she was always there for him, and for their kids, standing by Jack when things went badly at work, taking care of shuffling the kids back and forth when he had yet another out of town business meeting. And through it all, she'd loved him, lived for those fleeting moments when he gave her his attention. They were rare, but when they happened, they were unforgettable.

She'd been such a fool. All those years she'd struggled as a writer, putting her own career on the back burner while she nurtured his and took care of the children because he was too busy to do anything but work.

Now she was poised on the verge of success. Her agent told her a sale of her latest book to one of the big publishers looked promising. Very promising.

She allowed her first smile of the day.

"What are you grinning about?"

She jumped when Jack spoke, so immersed in her own thoughts she'd forgotten he stood nearby. He slid a plate in front of her and sat, occupying his usual chair that had stood empty for too many years. Now it was like the past five years had disappeared, as if they'd been some kind of dream and this was her reality now. A sense of comfort overcame her and she knew it was because Jack was here, smiling at her as if he'd never left.

Obviously she was still dreaming. This was no reality. "I was thinking about my latest book."

He scooped up a forkful of eggs, arching a brow as he swallowed. "Tell me how that's going."

"It's going great. I've sold a few books to a smaller publisher, but my agent has my latest and claims there's going to be a bidding war by some of the big names out there."

His beaming smile was like an arrow to her heart. "Always knew you could do it, Katie. You've always had amazing talent."

She sniffed. Yeah, right. As if he'd ever taken the time to even ask her what she was writing or take the slightest interest in her work. How would he know how talented she was? He'd never read a word of what she'd written.

"I've read every book you've written. You have a gift, Kate. An amazing gift that I'm so glad you're utilizing."

Good thing she was sitting down or she'd have fallen to the ground. Shock made her eyes widen and she nearly choked on the orange juice she'd just swallowed. "You've read my books?"

His smile was sheepish and he hunched his shoulders. "Yeah. I'm sorry it took me so long. You're incredible, Kate. I wish I hadn't been so selfish all those years so you'd have had more time to get your writing going. My leaving was actually the best thing for you. It made you write and submit your work."

She sat back and regarded him, unable to believe this was the same Jack who used to sit across the table from her, on the rare occasions he was actually home, of course, so engrossed in his newspaper he'd never know whether she was there or not. And when he wasn't busy with paperwork for his business, he was off on a trip. By the time he'd get home, he'd be exhausted and barely have time to spend with the boys, let alone inquire about her writing.

This Jack seemed relaxed, focusing all his attentions on her. She wasn't used to this version of her husband and didn't quite know how to react. Suspicious, she waited for him to launch into detailed explanations of what he'd been doing for the past five years, but so far, nothing about himself. Only about her.

Bizarre.

"You're looking at me funny."

She arched a brow. "Funny?"

"Yeah. Like you can't believe I'm really here."

Well, duh. What she couldn't believe was the version of Jack that sat across from her. "This is too weird. You know it as well as I do."

His lips curved into a grin. "Well, yeah, you could say that. But I'm here, so let's make the best of it and not question why."

Easy for him to say. He wasn't the one with questions.

And more questions, especially when he got up, cleared the table and did all the dishes. This had to be a dream! Jack never did domestic chores around the house. Ever.

"Let's go shopping."

She stared at him as if he spoke a foreign language. "Huh?"

"Shopping. Go take a shower, get dressed and let's go. Day-light's wasting."

Shock prevented her from objecting, especially when he grabbed her hands and hauled her to her feet. She stood and mutely allowed him to direct her down the hall toward the bath-room. She stepped into the hot shower, convinced she'd just dreamed the past couple hours and when she came out, she'd find Jack was still as gone as he had been the past five years.

But he wasn't. She dried her hair, dressed and opened the bed-room door. There he stood, looking completely edible and way too good-looking for her. She cringed at the thought of being seen with him in public.

Then again, they really didn't know anyone in town. The country house sat on over two acres of land overlooking the lake, and they mainly kept to themselves. The chances of running into anyone they knew in town were slim.

When they stepped outside, a brisk gust of wind caught her jacket and flung it open. She held it tightly closed with one hand and looked around the circular driveway.

"Uhhh, Jack, where's your car?"

"Don't have it anymore. I took a taxi out here."

"A taxi. From town?"

"Yeah. I grabbed your keys off the dresser. We'll take your car."

Stunned speechless, she slid in the car and buckled her seat belt. Jack never went anywhere without his expensive luxury sedan, his pride and joy, his status symbol of success. He'd never sell that car. And why didn't he have another car to drive?

"Jack, I don't under—"

"Why I'm going shopping with you?" he asked, cutting her off mid-question. "It's simple. I'm going to do all the things I never did with you before. All the things I claimed to be too busy to do. Like shopping and buying you things and spending time with you." He glanced at her and said, "I've missed just being with you, Katie. I've missed touching you, holding you and kissing you. I've missed pressing my body up against yours at night, breathing in the smell of your hair and skin. I miss all of that so much it makes me hurt inside."

Tears pooled in her eyes and she willed them away, turning quickly to look out the window. She would not fall for his charm again. Nothing he said mattered to her. In an hour or two he'd grow tired of this game and be off on a phone call or a trip. He may have had an attack of nostalgia and maybe a little guilt, but that didn't mean he'd come back to her. Not really.

She'd lost Jack forever a long time ago. Nothing he did or said now would bring back the man she once loved.

four

"ARE YOU INSANE?"

An hour into their shopping trip, Jack stood her in front of the town's trendiest hair salon.

"Of course I'm not insane. You're getting your hair and nails done today, and a pedicure. I'll wait."

"I am not getting anything done and you're crazy."

With eyes that sparkled like they had when he was young, he turned her toward the entrance of the salon where two smiling women waited to work on her. Hell, it would take them at least a week to make her look good.

"Go," he whispered, his warm breath caressing her neck and making goose bumps pop out all over her skin. "I'll be waiting for you. I'm not going anywhere, Katie, I promise."

I'm not going anywhere. Those words both chilled and warmed her during the two-hour hair and nail extravaganza. She expected at any moment to look up and find Jack had disappeared, but he hadn't. He sat in a chair at the front of the salon the entire time, reading magazines and occasionally glancing up to smile over at her.

The looks he gave her heated her from the inside out. The way

117

he used to look at her, before he got too busy to notice whether she was even in the room or not. Hot gazes filled with the promise of scorching sex.

The result was a complete biological meltdown. Her breasts ached and her nipples tightened. Her long-ignored pussy flamed to life, her clit quivering with the need to be touched, licked and sucked. She squirmed in her chair and tried to ignore her betraying body's signals to leap from her seat, straddle Jack and fuck his brains out before he left her again.

God, she missed sex with him. Even when they had reached the point where they'd become nearly strangers, when they came together at night it was explosive. They may have had a full list of problems, but sex had never been one of them.

All those old feelings of desire and need and want came crashing down over her with every one of his seductive glances. Damn him. She was supposed to hate him, not crave him.

His gaze caught and held hers, and she read the heat in his eyes. Something passed between them at that moment and she shivered. It had been a long time since he looked at her with barely controlled hunger in his eyes. And she wasn't immune, either. Her body was so in tune to him that it screamed from the inside out, waking with a sexual vengeance she wasn't prepared to handle.

"Okay, honey, you're all finished!"

Finally. She smiled apologetically at Mary, her hairdresser, who no doubt had to struggle with the messy mop on her head. But instead of looking disgusted, Mary beamed, winked and flipped Kate's chair around so she could look in the mirror.

Okay, *wow* was the first word that came to mind. Who was that woman in the mirror? Ten years had just been peeled away as she stared, openmouthed, at her reflection in the glass.

Two hours, a facial, eyebrow wax, haircut, color and makeup could not have made that drastic a change to her appearance. But it sure looked that way.

They'd chopped off at least six inches of lifeless hair, giving her a newer, trendier cut that skimmed just along her chin. The color was a deep, rich auburn, bringing out the amber in her eyes and highlighting her cheekbones.

The makeup they'd applied hadn't hurt, either. As a stay at home writer she usually wore her pajamas and no makeup. Since Jack left she'd had no reason to get dressed, do anything with her hair or go out unless she met the boys or had a meeting.

But this new hairstyle and makeup brightened her face like it hadn't been for . . . years. That had to be the reason she looked so much younger now.

"Get over there and show that hunky man of yours the new look," Mary suggested.

He wasn't *her* hunky man. Not any longer. Nevertheless, she stood and headed toward Jack, who was currently engrossed in a weekly gossip magazine, of all things. He looked up when she stopped in front of him, his eyes widening and his jaw dropping. She suppressed a smile at her purely feminine reaction to his look of shock and pleasure.

"Wow," he said, standing up and walking around her.

She felt more self-conscious than she ever had before, like Pygmalion's creation at the grand unveiling. Had she really looked so bad before? The answer was yes, she realized with a huge rush of embarrassment. How could she have let herself go that way?

Jack stopped in front of her again, took her hands and pulled her against him. The first contact of her nipples against his hard chest was electrifying. She stared into his eyes, knowing she should object, push away. Something to maintain a careful distance between them. But for the life of her she couldn't help but enjoy the way he looked at her right now.

"There's my girl," he whispered, slanting his lips across hers.

It was a simple, gentle brush of mouth to mouth, but in a heartbeat all was lost. She breathed in the scent of him, thrilled to the softness of his lips against hers, the way his body fit against hers as if they'd been made for each other. She was suddenly sixteen years old again, being kissed for the very first time by the boy she'd fantasized about for years. Her relationship with Jack went so far back she couldn't remember a time he wasn't part of her life.

Which had made his abrupt departure so much worse.

Cruel reality intruded into her moment of nostalgic bliss and she placed her palms on his chest, gently pushing away. Her lips tingled, her nipples beading against her bra and her panties moistening. In an instant she'd forgotten everything he'd done to her, the years of feeling betrayed by his broken promises. How easily she'd been seduced by male appreciation for surface appearance.

Jack searched her face and she realized he knew her thoughts.

"I know. I still have a lot to make up for, Katie. You don't trust in my love and I don't blame you for your lack of faith. One step at a time, okay?"

She nodded, wary but willing to keep an open mind.

"Let's go shopping," he said.

He took her hand and led her out of the salon and into the town's trendiest clothing boutique. It was small and very, very expensive. She'd never been one to spend money on clothes, especially those that came with a price tag she could feed her family a month on.

"Why are you doing this?" she asked as he led her to the evening wear.

"Because I have to. I need to. I want to shower you with gifts and attention and everything you missed out on all those years because I was such a selfish bastard."

She couldn't argue with the selfish bastard part. "I don't need any new clothes."

"You have anything at the house to wear to go dancing at the country club?"

Country club? Who was he kidding? They weren't even members there. "Jack, we don't even belong—"

"We do now. Come on. Let's go see what they have in here."

They were greeted by a very tall, statuesque blonde who couldn't be more than twenty-five. She smiled enthusiastically and led them to the cocktail dress section, no doubt smelling a sale. A big sale.

Hell, one outfit here could feed an entire third-world country for a month! But Jack insisted, grasping her hand and dragging her around while Suzie the salesclerk brought out a stack of dresses.

None of those dresses would either fit or look good on her. They were too short, too tight and would reveal way too much of everything she was desperate to conceal. But Jack chose five dresses and all but pushed her into the dressing room to try them on.

"I've also brought some undergarments and shoes to go with these dresses," Suzie enthused, then shut the door and left Kate alone. She stared at the dresses and then her reflection in the mirror.

Too tight blue jeans and a bulky sweater did nothing for her figure. Then again, they suited her lifestyle. Those . . . things . . . hanging up in the room were not her and it was about time she made her choices clear to Jack and Suzie both. She turned and opened the door, stepping out and running smack into Jack's chest.

"Oh, no, you don't," he said, pushing her backward and shutting the door behind him. "I thought you might try to make an escape. I'm here to see you don't."

"You're not supposed to be in here!" she hissed.

He waved a hand toward the door and shrugged. "Oh, Suzie doesn't care. She knows if she sells at least one of those dresses she's going to make a bundle. Now try them on."

"I will not." Especially with him standing in the room with her. He hadn't seen her naked in five years. Well, longer than that considering they hadn't had much sex at the end and when they had it had typically been in the dark. No way was she going to let him see what her body looked like now.

"If you don't take your clothes off, I'm going to do it for you."

His threat sent her mind careening into visuals she had no business visualizing. Like Jack peeling layer by layer of clothing from her body, touching his hot mouth to every spot he revealed. The room temperature increased by ten degrees and she broke out into a sweat. She could call his bluff, but the determined expression on his face told her he wasn't kidding about undressing her. "Get out, Jack. I'll try the damn outfits on, but not with you standing in here."

He tilted his head to the side, then nodded. "I'll be right outside the door. Just holler when you have one on and I'll come take a look."

Great. Just what she needed. Why was she even allowing herself to be pulled, prodded, and forced in a direction she didn't want to go, anyway?

She knew the reason. Because deep down . . . really deep down . . . she wanted this. Maybe it was a challenge to see if she could somehow squeeze her body into one, just one of these gorgeous dresses. She hadn't worn anything pretty in years and it was about damn time she made some changes.

If only she had the body to match the dresses, she could really show Jack what he'd given up when he left.

She wanted to hurt him. The realization hit like an icy chill on a wintry day. She wanted him to feel the same pain she'd felt when he left, to realize that maybe what he'd left hadn't been so bad after all, that maybe, just maybe, he should have worked a little harder to stay.

Get over yourself, Kate. He left for a damn good reason and you know it. Quit trying to make it something it isn't.

With a heavy sigh she struggled out of her jeans and sweater, then removed her underwear, refusing to even glance in the direction of the full-length mirror while she slipped into decadent underthings. Lord, it was amazing they fit her. She chose the dress she liked best. A black, slinky, clingy short cocktail dress that hugged every one of her curves. What the hell, it was good for a laugh before she took it off, right? Smoothing the matching black hose against her legs, she slipped into the heels and braced herself for disappointment when she turned around.

"You still in there?" she heard Jack say through the door.

She froze and stared at the door. "Yeah."

"I'm coming in."

"Wait!" But before she could reach out to lock the door, he'd opened it.

"Holy shit, Kate," he whispered, his gaze traveling from her eyes down to her feet.

He was being kind. Okay, he scored points for that. "Thanks. Gimme a minute and I'll slip another of these dresses on."

"What the hell for? You got me hard in a second just looking at you in that thing. Jesus Christ, Katie!"

She rolled her eyes at him. "Give me a break, Jack. I look like a sausage."

"Have you looked in the mirror yet?"

"No." And she planned to slip off this dress and put on another without once turning around to stare at herself in the mirror. Mirrors revealed all flaws, especially dressing room mirrors.

He grasped her shoulders and turned her around. "Then take a peek so you can see what I see."

Ugh. She didn't want to, but she had no choice when he fully spun her around. She looked down at her feet first, not recognizing the slim ankles and shapely calves that led up to slender thighs and . . .

"Oh my God!"

five

WHO WAS THAT woman in the mirror? Not the same one she'd seen last night, that was certain. Was she hallucinating? The lighting in the dressing room couldn't be that good.

But she definitely looked . . . different. The dress clung to her, all right, but she didn't look fat or out of shape. The snug fabric slenderized her shape and showed off all her curves.

Well, okay. Her curves were a bit ample. Hell, she wasn't twenty-five anymore. What did she expect?

"You've always been overly critical of yourself," Jack whispered as if he'd heard her internal thoughts. "You look hot as hell, Katie. Delectable. I'd like to eat you alive, right here."

There went the temp in the room, notched up another ten degrees. Good thing the dress was sleeveless. What kind of game was he playing with her? Before, he'd never noticed whether she'd been dressed in sweatpants or an evening gown with a tiara on her head.

"You've never seen what I see in you," he said, stepping behind her and resting his hands on the curve of her hips. Her skin burned at his light touch.

"You stopped looking at me a long time ago," she shot back at his reflection in the mirror, irritated that he was giving her the full-court press. He had to be after something. Some ulterior motive for his oddly attentive behavior. But what?

He frowned, his lids half closing. Then he looked up and met her gaze head-on. "I never stopped looking. I was just . . . I don't know what happened to me, Kate. Somewhere along the way I lost sight of what was important. You, the boys, everything that should have mattered. I told you I screwed up. I've spent the past five years thinking of nothing but that, wondering if you realized how much better off you were without me causing you such pain."

"Leaving me caused me more pain that I thought I could bear." But she *had* borne it, had survived it, had learned to live with the sense of betrayal and mistrust ever since the day he left. "Why did you come back, Jack?"

"To appreciate you the way I never did before. To make you appreciate yourself the way you never did. Beyond your surface beauty, there's a kind, gentle heart that always gave and gave and gave without hesitation, while I took and took and took. You were always there for me, Katie. Me and the boys. You were unselfish and loving with a hundred percent of your heart and soul, and that's what makes you beautiful to me."

His words knifed through her middle, making her ache to turn around and throw her arms around him. But she held back, the part of her that still hurt hesitant to allow her to open her heart again.

He bent his head and pressed a soft kiss to the side of her neck. Her nipples tightened against the snug fabric of the dress as, despite her irritation at him, her body responded with a wild flare of desire.

"I don't need you to appreciate me." But the words sounded as hollow as they felt. She *did* need him to appreciate her, more than she could admit to herself.

"Yes, you do. Now look at yourself and let me tell you what I see."

"I don't want to play this game, Jack."

"It's not a game. I'm serious. Look."

She did, meeting his gaze in the mirror, forcing herself to face who she really was now.

"Your face has a glow about it. That always mesmerized me about you. The way your eyes light up when you smile and your cheeks turn pink when you're embarrassed. Do you remember how shy you were when we first met?"

"Yes." She'd almost died when he'd asked her out the first time, sure he was playing some kind of joke on her. He was a senior football player and she was a geeky, gawky sophomore who hadn't a clue how to act around boys. But he'd been kind and gentle, never pressuring her for more than she was ready to give. And she'd fallen hopelessly in love with him. He'd been her first love. Her only love.

"The way you used to smile at me when you thought I wasn't looking drove me crazy. God I loved that yearning in your eyes, Katie. That sweet innocence in those warm eyes that made me want to take care of you and protect you forever. I fell in love with your eyes first, and I still love them best about you. They tell me everything you're feeling."

She studied her reflection as if she could see any telltale signs in her eyes. They had a dark, honeyed look to them right now, as if there was molten fire behind them. Is that what Jack saw when he looked at her? Were her emotions always that transparent?

Memories did that to her. Made her remember all the good times, instead of concentrating on the bad times like she should be doing.

JACI BURTON

His hand on her hip caught her attention. Squeezing gently, he caressed the curve from waist to thigh, his breath hot against her neck as he bent down to pet her body. "You know, I love your eyes, but there's a lot more. Especially the way you feel under my hands." He pressed his palm against her hip. "I love this part of you. Every curve in your body entices me. I'd like to undress you and lay you out naked in the sunlight so I could study every inch of you."

She cringed at the thought of every bump of cellulite exposed to the glaring sun.

His laugh was husky and dark, his chest rumbling against her back. Her legs trembled. "You always thought I scrutinized every flaw. I don't. I adore the perfection of you. You are an amazing creature, Katherine Mary McKay. From your remarkable intelligence to the fierce way you protected our sons to the unselfish way you gave up everything so I could do my job. It will take an eternity for me to repay you for all you did for me, and even that won't be enough."

This side of Jack was so new, so unexpected, that she was at a loss for words. A snappy comeback to an empty promise was easy. But she heard sincerity in his words, and a depth of his soul he'd never revealed to her before.

He kissed her shoulder, drawing one thin strap down her arm, his fingers blazing a trail of sensual promise that made her shiver despite the heat in the small dressing room. Thoughts of anger and betrayal fled as her body tuned in completely to his touch, his scent, the way his hard body felt pressed against her.

"Let me love you, Kate," he whispered, drawing the other strap down and pulling the dress to her waist. The black bra lifted her breasts and squeezed them together, offering an enticing bit of cleavage.

Jack moved his hands in front of her, caressing the swell of her breasts. "You always had beautiful breasts, babe. So full and soft. And your nipples, now those are a work of art." He drew the straps of her bra down and pulled the fabric away from the mounds. Her breasts fell into his hands and he cupped them, using his thumbs to draw circles around the pink areolas, tantalizing them with unbearably soft strokes until she gasped. He circled the distended nipples, plucking gently at first, then a little harder.

Watching him touch her was embarrassing and yet so erotic her panties flooded with cream. She'd definitely have to buy the underwear now.

"Jack, please," she begged, not sure whether to plead for him to stop touching her in public or urge him to fuck her right here. She had no idea what she wanted, and was tired of thinking. It had been too damn long since she'd been touched, too long without feeling alive and desirable. She deserved this moment and to hell with how she *should* feel!

His hands worked magic on her breasts and nipples, firing her libido to life in a wickedly tortuous way. He licked her neck, scraping his teeth along the side of it to take a bite from her nape. She shuddered and backed against him, instinct driving her ass against the rigid bulge in his jeans.

"You make me so fucking hard, Kate," he ground out. She switched her gaze from the movement of his hands to his face. His jaw was clenched tight and a bead of sweat formed along his temple.

A sizeable erection was evident in the firm swell pressed against her buttocks. Her throat went dry. But the rest of her was wet. Hot and wet. He rocked against her and more moisture spilled from her pussy lips onto her panties.

"I smell you," he said, licking her neck like he thirsted and she was his drink. "I've missed that sweet smell of sex, that sweet scent of you when you're hot and wet and needy for me."

He trailed his right hand over her rib cage and abdomen, pausing to squeeze her hip before moving down to the hem of her dress. He bunched the fabric in his hand and yanked upward, revealing the decadent stockings she'd slipped on earlier. The black garter belt was hot. Even she thought so, revealing only a smidgeon of the pale skin of her thighs peeking between her panties and the stockings.

"Ah, Christ, Katie." He jerked the dress all the way up, then moved around to face her. His expression was tight, fierce, almost as if he was angry and trying to hold it in. He pulled her against him, his mouth crashing down over hers.

He took, he ravaged, plunging his tongue between her parted lips and fucking her mouth with an intensity that left her breathless. She moaned at the sheer exquisiteness of tasting him again, familiarity as exciting as the newness of his bold domination of her. She clutched his shirt, her nails digging into his chest as he drew her even closer. His erection rasped against her swollen clit, shooting off sparks and flooding her with more of her juices. She'd never wanted like this before, not even in the beginning.

Now she was starving for it, for Jack, desperate to grab onto whatever fleeting moments they could have together, no longer caring that she was supposed to hate him for what he'd done. She palmed his cock and caressed the part of him she was desperate to feel embedded deep inside her.

"No," he said, his voice rough with passion. "Not yet." He dropped to his knees, his gaze locked with hers, and reached for the thin straps of her panties. With agonizingly slow movements, he dragged them down her hips and legs, each brush of the silken fabric against her skin making her grit her teeth in anticipation.

She held onto his shoulder as she stepped out of the panties, shocked when Jack held them to his nose and inhaled, his eyes closing for a second. When he opened them, the gray orbs had darkened like a pitch-black night. "I love the smell of your pussy, Kate. Just the scent of you makes me so fucking hard I could come in my pants right now."

Her knees buckled and she squeezed his shoulder for support. But he withdrew her hand, backing her up against the door and following her on his knees. He spread her legs apart, lifting one over his shoulder. Like this, her pussy was right in line with his face. He studied her, tilting his head from one side to another, then breathing deeply as if he couldn't get enough of her aroused scent.

His words were whispered, his voice a gravelly softness that curled her toes. "Do you want to come, Katie? Right here? You want me to eat that sweet pussy until you have to bite your tongue to keep from screaming, don't you?"

God help her, she couldn't hold the words back. "Yes!"

Six

I⊤ HAD BEEN too long since she'd been touched. When Jack's hands cupped her buttocks and drew her closer to his mouth, his hot breath teasing the curls covering her sex, she knew she was going to embarrass herself by coming almost immediately. He leaned his forehead against her belly and stilled, breathing heavily.

Was he having trouble maintaining control? Cool, calm collected Jack McKay was ruffled? Amazing. But then she heard it, a low growl coming from his throat, so primitive and arousing her pussy responded with a quaking shudder, a welcoming call of the wild.

He dipped down and licked through the curls on her mound, nipping at her with his teeth. She had nothing to hold onto and was afraid her legs wouldn't hold her, especially when she felt the warm wetness of his tongue along her folds. Unbidden, a moan escaped her lips. Reaching for his head, she tangled her fingers in his hair, closed her eyes and held on.

The spark was lit with the first swipe of his tongue against her clit. When he covered the bud with his lips and teased it with his tongue, she burst into an inferno, forcing herself to hold onto sanity and not come yet. Not yet. The pleasure was too great, the sensations too exquisite to let go so quickly.

She opened her eyes and watched him perform his magic. His tongue swirled over the swollen hood to lap at the hard pearl underneath. Before she could shriek from the sheer bliss of such an intimate touch, he'd moved further south, licking along her slit, forcing her pussy lips open so he could slide his tongue inside and lap the cream pouring from her.

It was decadent, wicked, and so damned arousing she sobbed out a whimper. Jack tilted his head back and she saw the half smile on his lips before his tongue blazed a hot, wet trail back to her clit.

"Jack," she whispered, knowing she had nothing to say to him, but still needing him to know that his mouth was magic.

She'd always craved his touch, even when things between them had become distant. Long after he'd left she'd lived in a state of shock that she would never feel the warmth of his hands gliding along her skin, or the magic of his mouth when he kissed her and loved her in this most intimate way.

And now he was back and she didn't care why or for how long. She needed this. No, that wasn't quite right. It went far beyond need. She demanded it, and nothing would stop her from getting what she wanted.

"There," she directed, holding his head in place when his tongue found that magical spot she knew would send her over the edge. But he'd already stilled and focused his attention on that location. She heard his dark laugh of satisfaction, reveled in the intimacy of the man who knew her so well she didn't have to lead him to find her sweet spot.

Release hovered close, teasing and tormenting her. A sweet bliss she craved but wanted to hold back. If she only had this one time she was going to make it last forever.

But he tortured her incessantly, swirling his tongue in circles around her throbbing clit. When he reached up and slid his finger along her folds, then inserted it into her pussy, she felt the contractions in her womb, bit the inside of her cheek to keep from crying out and let the sensations overtake her.

Her orgasm raged through her like a sudden tidal wave, crest after crest battering her body until it shook uncontrollably. She held onto Jack like a life preserver, clutching her fingers in his hair while he continued to fuck her with his finger. Never once did he stop, even when the vibrations became unbearable. She floated briefly before riding the wave to another crashing climax that left her panting and unable to stand.

He rose and covered her mouth with his, letting her taste the sweet release she'd poured onto his tongue. She met his kiss with all the passion she'd held inside, needing to feel one with him, a part of him. Needing him inside her like she'd never needed before.

Jack tore his mouth from hers and laid his forehead against hers, panting heavily.

"We'll finish this later. When I fuck you I want all the time in the world, not just a few minutes."

She felt cold when he stepped away from her. Cold and suddenly feeling exposed way more than physically. What was wrong with her? Five years of gloomy depression simply disappeared with one touch of his tongue to her clit? Was she really that easy, that gullible?

Yes, Jack seemed different in so many ways, but what guarantees did she have that he wouldn't disappear again? The thought of it made her want to curl up in a ball and scream. She doubted she'd survive it a second time, and yet she'd let him back in so easily.

Stupid, stupid, stupid. You're supposed to enjoy the moment and not let your heart get involved. But she'd given it all to him once again, baring her heart and soul for his taking.

And there he stood in front of her, his gaze hot and filled with wild desire, and she wanted to offer herself up to him again.

It's just a dream, Kate. Don't think too much. Go with it, enjoy it, but hold your heart closed.

She could do this. Really, she could. He couldn't possibly hurt her more than he already had, so why not take a little from him this time? God knows she desperately needed what he was offering.

She was nearly naked and he was still fully clothed, standing there staring at her as she fought for control over her limbs. But how could she stop trembling with the way he looked at her? Heat fused her core at the look of raw need in his eyes, the way his jaw clenched tight and his hands balled into fists.

Jack fought for control. He wanted her, the evidence clearly outlined against his jeans. But he held back. Waiting. And she could, too. Dressing quickly, she hurried from the dressing room, hoping the telltale blush on her cheeks and her mussed hair wouldn't give away what they'd been doing in there.

Suzie was thankfully oblivious as Jack placed the outfit she'd worn onto the counter and paid for it, all the while exchanging hot glances with Kate that melted her into a puddle of arousal right there in the middle of the store.

Though she knew him well, had known him her entire life, he looked at her now as if he saw her for the first time, had just tasted her for the first time, and wanted more.

Dammit, she shouldn't, but she liked these feelings he evoked in her. She liked the newness of it all, as if they were just starting a relationship. Deep down she knew that whatever was happening between them wasn't permanent. Despite the allure of rediscovered sex, she had to force herself to remember that.

He's not staying. Don't let your heart get wrapped up in this.

Jack had returned to atone for his abrupt departure, in some way asking for forgiveness. But he didn't fool her one bit. He'd never said he'd come back permanently. So she'd just enjoy the moment and when he left again, she'd get over it. She'd done it before. Surely it couldn't hurt as much the second time as it had the first, right?

Right.

Now if only she could really believe that.

Ah, the hell with it. He owed her. She was going to take it.

They drove back to the house to shower and change for dinner. Kate felt strange putting on the dress and sexy lingerie again, all too aware of what had happened the last time she wore it. But they were going to the country club for dinner. He couldn't very well ravage her in the middle of the dining room in front of hundreds of people, could he?

Though the idea had some appeal.

She giggled as she fastened her earrings and gazed at the finished product in the bathroom mirror. Shaking her head, her hair swept sexily from side to side, little wisps caressing her cheek as she moved.

She looked . . . hot. Giggling again, she slipped on her shoes and went out to look for Jack. He was in the living room string out the bay windows toward the lake, his back turned to her. Dressed in a long-sleeved shirt and black slacks that framed his well-sculpted ass, she swallowed past the desert in her throat.

Screw dinner. She wanted to have Jack for dinner. His cock in her mouth for an appetizer, a heady sixty-nine for the main course and a nice, long fuck for dessert.

She shuddered at the visual of being spread out on the carpet underneath the big window, the setting sun a backdrop for some glorious, sweaty sex.

But instead, she sighed and asked, "You ready?"

He turned to her and she sucked in a breath. Still so damned handsome her heart stopped whenever she looked at him. The way he smiled at her reminded her of when they were young and first fell in love. That smile held a promise of forever. Funny she should see it grace his face now.

"I'm ready. And you're gorgeous. Shall we go?" He held out his arm and she stepped toward him, sliding her hand into the crook and feeling every bit like Cinderella on her way to the ball.

But Cinderella always knew the stroke of midnight would change things, her fantasy would vanish right before her eyes. Kate would do well to remember that too. Anything magical was fleeting at best. Just like her time with Jack.

"How did you get into the country club?" she asked as they arrived in front of the expansive, one-story Pleasantville Country Club. The golf course was visible from the front porch of their country house and they'd often laughed about how one day they'd be rich enough to afford the ridiculously expensive entry fee.

Another "one day" that had never happened.

"I have connections," he said as he helped her out of the car and tossed the keys to the valet.

Kate went silent as they walked up the marble steps toward the lobby door. Connections. Right. What kind of connections did he have now that he hadn't had five years ago? When he left, he'd given her everything, including his business. She'd sold the business and used the money to live on while she worked on her writing career. Hell, why not? He'd abandoned everything and left it all to her to deal with. At least he'd left her something of value.

There were still so many questions. Why wasn't she grilling him about where he'd been, what he'd been doing and the most important question of all . . . why was he back?

Because you don't really want to know the answers.

The truth of that statement hovered around her like the growing night mist swirling in the air. She cast it aside and preferred oblivious ignorance to knowing the truth.

The country club was everything she'd always imagined it would be. Multiple crystal chandeliers graced the cathedral ceiling of the ballroom-sized dining room, their sparkle like glittering diamonds. Parquet flooring led onto rich, thick carpet colored a soft grey and blue. An expansive dance floor centered hundreds of round tables outfitted with white linen tablecloths and fine china and silver.

They were so far out of their league here she almost laughed, but didn't want to call attention to herself. Though no one looked their way as the hostess led them to their table. They could be invisible for all the attention they gathered. Which suited her just fine. At any moment she expected a tap on the shoulder followed by an announcement that they weren't allowed to stay.

A very attentive waiter brought them wine, took their food order and acted as if they truly belonged in this opulent lifestyle of the rich. Whatever. If Jack paid them a bundle to get them in for the evening, so be it. She was going to enjoy the food, the drink and dance her heart out.

For tomorrow it could all be gone.

And no one knew that better than her.

Seven

"Have I told you tonight how beautiful you look?"

No more than about a hundred times, she mused. But she wasn't complaining. "Thank you, Jack."

They'd eaten and had wine, enjoying conversation about the boys and her life since he'd left. Not once had he offered an explanation about the past five years, nor had he given her an inkling to what would happen in their future.

A small part of her wanted, needed to know the answers. A large part of her wanted to stay in the moment and quit worrying about things she had no control over.

Certainly a new and improved version of herself, that was certain. But why not? Jack wasn't going to stay. He was here to wine her, dine her and give her screaming orgasms for as long as he deigned to remain. She was going to sit back and let him.

Hell, for all she knew she could still be dreaming. If she was, then she could do anything, be anything, act any way she wanted to and it wouldn't matter in the light of day what had happened in her dreams.

"Dance with me."

When was the last time they'd danced together? He stood and

held out his hand. Smiling, she slipped her palm against his and followed him onto the dance floor.

Their favorite song played, an old fifties song about romance and finding the love of your life. As she stared into the unfathomable eyes of the man she'd loved forever, her heart clenched and tears pooled in her eyes.

"I've missed you, Jack," she finally admitted out loud. "So much."

He allowed her a fleeting glimpse of the pain in his eyes before he shielded them and smiled. "I've missed you too, Katie. I've thought of you every day, every night, wishing I could go back and change everything. I would, you know, if I could."

She believed him. "I know. It's enough that you're here now. Let's not talk about what neither of us can change."

He nodded and pulled her against him, her softness against his rock-hard solid strength. More than anything, she missed this feeling of protectiveness, of knowing nothing bad could happen to her as long as Jack held her in his arms.

They swayed together, oblivious to the other couples dancing around them. Kate laid her head on his shoulder, absorbing his scent, the comforting strength of his hard chest against her breast and the feel of his body under her hands.

Time suspended, memories washing over her so fast she couldn't keep up with the visions coursing through her mind. From the beginning . . . the first time he kissed her, the first time they made love, their wedding, the birth of the boys . . . everything came rushing back to her. At that moment she knew exactly what she wanted.

"Take me home, Jack. Make love to me."

He drew back and searched her face, his eyes turning dark. He nodded and led her to the car. The drive home was made in silence, but he held her hand the entire time, his thumb rubbing against her fingers.

Kate watched the way his hand moved over hers, memorizing every stroke of his thumb, committing the feel of his touch to memory. Before, she hadn't been prepared for his departure. This time she would be. Like a clock ticking in her head, she knew the countdown had started. Somehow, part of her knew that her time with Jack was fleeting.

Maybe that was part of this dream. Spending nights with him, letting her imagination run wild into scenarios of "what if," trying out how she'd react if he ever really did come back to her. The safe haven of her imagination allowed her to break free of the anger and hurt and truly live again in the arms of the man she loved.

Jack pulled up in front of the house, turned off the ignition and got out, making his way to her side of the car. Everything that happened after that seemed like a slow-motion play on a movie. He opened the door, lifted her out with both hands, then swept her into his arms, taking the steps two at a time. She tilted her head back and laughed when he stood on the porch and twirled her around in circles. She was dizzy, ecstatic and crazy in love with him. Unlocking the chains around her heart made her soar with freedom again. Even if this was a dream, it was a catharsis, a reawakening she'd desperately needed.

Nudging the door open with his shoulder, he kicked it closed with his foot, driving his mouth down hard against hers as soon as she heard the click of the door lock. She tangled her fingers in his hair and pulled him closer, desperate to feel no barriers between them except their own needs and desires.

In an instant she was on her feet, Jack's hands sweeping around her and drawing her hips against his. His cock was erect, hot and thick. He rocked against her and her sex wept with need for him. A whimper escaped her throat when his hand found her breast, kneading her flesh and scraping his thumb against her nipple.

Too many clothes separated his hand from her skin. "Jack, please," she begged, thrusting her breast into his hand.

He laughed, the sound low and husky and driving her arousal to a near fevered pitch. He lifted her and carried her into the bedroom, turning on the small table lamp. Soft light filtered the room, not too much to glare harshly, but enough that they could see each other.

Typically she'd want the light off, not wanting him to see the way her body had changed. But after today in the dressing room, it was pointless to try and hide the ravages of time. Besides, she thought with a soft curl of her lips, he thought she was beautiful.

He set her down on the bed and stepped away. The light shined behind him, casting his face in a dusky glow, silhouetting his body. And oh what a body! He yanked the tie from around his neck and began to slip each button from its hold. Shrugging out of his shirt, he stood and stared at her while she nearly drooled over his chest and flat abdomen, amazed that a man his age could still make her juices flow uncontrollably.

Truthfully, he looked about thirty-five. Tanned, well-muscled with a healthy glow that suffused his entire body. Dark hairs without a single gray among them scattered across his chest and lower, leading to a soft down of black fur that teased her by disappearing into the waistband of his pants.

She stood and reached for his belt, keeping her focus on his face. Slipping the belt loose, she popped the button on his pants. When she tugged the zipper down, her knuckles brushed his erection and he swore softly, moving his hips forward.

"Touch me, Katie. It's been too long."

She nodded and drew his pants down his hips, dropping to her knees to gaze at his cock. Thick, pulsing, the head engorged and dark, a pearl-sized drop of fluid lingered at the slit. She leaned forward and swiped her tongue over it, then covered her mouth over the head and sucked him inside.

"Christ!" he cried out, holding her face and slowly thrusting forward until his shaft was buried between her lips. She lapped at his cock head and swirled her tongue around and over the shaft, cupping his balls and massaging them while she loved his cock with her mouth.

His body trembled. The power to pleasure him was an amazing thing. To realize that he needed to be close to her, as much as she needed the same from him, made her love him more than she ever thought possible.

The soft sacs under his shaft tightened, drawing close to his body as she engulfed his cock deep into her mouth. She stroked the base of the shaft, propelling it between her lips, then drawing it out to lick the head, making sure he watched the movements of her tongue and lips. He uttered soft curses and kept his hands on her head, guiding her mouth over his shaft again and again.

She could do this all night long, but Jack pulled her to her feet and kissed her, parting the seam of her lips with his tongue. He swept it inside her mouth, thrusting and withdrawing until she was all but weeping with the need to feel those same motions inside her quaking pussy.

Jack pulled away and yanked at the straps of her dress, drawing them down her arms. The bra soon followed after he impatiently tore it away from her body, baring her breasts to his hungry gaze. He devoured her, first with his eyes, then with his hands, and finally, blissfully, with his mouth, tugging one nipple with his teeth while plucking the other with his fingers.

Her legs trembled and she held onto his shoulders for support. His pursuit of her body was purposeful and relentless. There wasn't a part of her he failed to touch as he slowly unveiled her skin, inch by inch, finally drawing her dress down over her hips and to the floor. She stepped out of her shoes and away from the dress, then stood there and waited for him to remove her garter belt, stockings and panties.

But he pushed her backward and she fell onto the bed. Jack followed, positioning her so her head was propped up on the pillows. He knelt between her spread legs, reached for the dainty panties and graced her with a devilish grin. With one quick jerk of his hands he ripped them off. A flood of cream poured from her slit. She'd never seen him like this before. His face was dark, dangerous, his jaw clenched tight and his lips pressed together. He used to look like that when he was deep into a project. Now he looked at *her* that way, as if she was the only thing that existed in his world.

"You have the most beautiful pussy I've ever seen," he murmured, studying her sex as if seeing it for the first time. He ran his fingers up and down her slit until she whimpered at the exquisite torture. "Pink, with plump, juicy lips that I'm dying to bury my dick between. Do you know how much I want to be inside you, Katie?"

To prove his point, he pushed back and took his shaft in his hand, clasping his fingers around the thick rod and stroking from base to tip. His eyes rolled back and he let out a soft groan. With his free hand he roamed her sex, patting her clit. Hot sparks shot deep inside her womb, melting her from the inside out. He tormented her, stroking himself and her at the same time, showing her his cock but not letting her have it.

"Dammit, Jack, please!" She didn't care that she begged. If he didn't fuck her and soon, she'd push him onto his back, straddle and ride him until the pressure inside her exploded. Then she'd take him along for the ride. She wanted his cum inside her.

He slipped two fingers between her pussy lips and buried them inside her cunt, pulling them out and fucking them in again, deeper and harder this time. Her pussy was soaked, cream running down the crack of her ass. She lifted her hips, driving her sex against his hand, clenching the coverlet in a death grip as she rode his fingers toward her impending orgasm.

"Oh, no," he said, withdrawing his fingers. He lifted her legs and pushed them backward, nestling his hips against her thighs. With one quick thrust he buried his thick wonderful cock all the way inside her. "When you come this time, I'll be in you, feeling your pussy shudder and grip my dick, forcing me to come with you."

Exactly what she wanted. She tugged at his hair and drew his face close to hers, needing the full contact of his body against every inch of hers he could possibly touch. The years apart dissolved, the pain with it, as they became one for the first time in a very long time.

When they'd been young, it had been hurried, both of them too inexperienced to understand the pleasure of taking their time. As they'd gotten older and had the boys, it had continued to be fast and furious. There had always been something else that needed their attention. Then his work had gotten in the way and sex had been an afterthought, a quick tumble to ease the tension, but somewhere along the way they'd lost the romance of making love.

Now they had time and used it to their advantage. Jack teased her clit, brushing his pelvis up and against her, then withdrew his cock until just the head remained inside her. She ran her fingers over his skin, digging her nails into his flesh when he didn't give her the intensity she needed.

"Fuck me, Jack," she demanded.

"As you wish," he teased.

It seemed to last forever, this giving and taking. His mouth devoured hers, at once hard and passionate and yet achingly tender. His cock did the same, moving slowly and gently at first, then hard and pounding as her need rose higher and higher. Jack seemed to instinctively know just where to take her, finally pushing her knees toward her head and pounding relentlessly, slamming so hard inside her that his balls slapped her ass. She welcomed it eagerly, wanting to hold him there for an eternity and never let him go.

But release loomed ever closer and try as she might, she couldn't hold it back. Like an oncoming train, it came faster and faster, careening toward her until she couldn't run from it anymore.

"Jack, I'm coming!" she cried out, her voice ragged. The answering cry was his as he jettisoned hot cum deep into her pussy, dragging her into a crashing orgasm that tore her in two. She cried, knew she drew blood as she buried her fingernails in his back, but she was helpless to stop. Pleasure like she'd never known before swept her into a frenzy. Tears rolled down her cheeks as she screamed again, a second, more powerful orgasm shooting through her like lightning, melting her from the inside out.

When she could finally feel his weight on top of her, could feel her trembling legs lowering onto the mattress, could feel their bodies entwined in the moist sweat of their own frantic lovemaking, she knew that what had just happened was special.

He held her against him, stroking her hair and her skin, pressing light kisses to the top of her head. Her heart squeezed painfully and she fought back the melancholy that threatened to overwhelm her.

Dreams were a magical link to her desires, and she knew there was a reason she'd dreamed of him every night. But what she experienced now was no dream and hadn't been since Jack had reappeared in her life. It was time to stop living in a fantasy world of her own making and face the reality of what was happening.

She'd been given an amazing gift, and no matter how much it hurt, she wouldn't rail at the injustice of it all.

But not yet. She needed a little while longer to feel him against her, to commit every touch, every look, every kiss to her memory.

Sometime later they still stroked each other, still kissed each other, and Kate could no longer hold her questions in silence.

Despite the tenuous hold they had on each other right now, she had to know.

"Jack?"

"Yeah?"

"Why did you leave me?"

He rolled over onto his back and took her with him, cradling her against his side. Her head rested on the left side of his chest, and she knew as soon as she lay her ear against it what she'd hear.

Nothing.

"I had to leave, Katie. It wasn't my choice. But I didn't want to. You know I didn't. Not with so much left unsettled. I had things left to do. Mistakes I made with you that I didn't have enough time to fix." He sighed and squeezed her hand. "You know, you always think you have all the time in the world to do the things you want to do. I wish I had known what was going to happen in time to fix it. But I didn't. Or maybe I did. Hell, I don't know now.

Maybe I saw the signs and ignored them. But I swear I didn't know about my bad heart, about how the years of stress and over-work would take their toll."

She lifted her head and looked deeply into his eyes, seeing the sorrow, the regret, knowing that the past five years had been as miserable for him as they'd been for her.

"I didn't know I was going to die, Kate."

Neither did she. But he had. Without warning. Just like that, he was gone. One day he was fine, the next he was dead. The doctor told her that the heart attack was devastating, that he had to have felt some pain for weeks or months beforehand.

But he hadn't said a word. Instead, he'd died at the office after working late one night. Leaving so much unsaid and unfinished between them.

"Is that why you're back? To make up for all you didn't do before you died?"

"Yes. I wasn't finished, Katie. Not with you, not by a long shot. I wanted that forever with you that we'd talked about. I hated that I'd allowed myself to get so sidetracked. I hated that all we planned for was ripped away because I was too stupid to recognize the signs."

She couldn't believe she was even having this conversation. But she was. And whether she believed in it or not, it had happened.

This was no dream at all. She'd just spent an amazingly glorious day and night with her dead husband.

Eight

THEY STAYED CURLED together for the longest time, neither of them saying a word. Kate held tight, afraid to move or say anything that would cause him to vanish from her life again. Somehow she knew what was coming and wasn't ready to face it yet.

Not yet, not when she'd just gotten him back.

"I can't stay, Katie."

She sat up and looked at him, nodding. She'd known that from the first. How, she had no idea. She'd just known that whatever this was, whatever had happened, was only temporary. If she thought she had to be strong five years ago, she was wrong. Now she needed that inner strength more than ever, because she knew that no matter what she wanted, she'd have to let him go. She'd been given a gift, and she was damn lucky to have gotten this much. "I know."

He reached for her hand and brought it to his lips, kissing every knuckle and every finger. "I wish I could. God, I wish I could. You have to believe me. Funny how we never seem to appreciate what we love the most until we don't have it anymore. Why is that?"

Which was why she'd held onto the feelings of betrayal and anger for so long. They'd protected her from hurt, from her own guilt at not insisting that he slow down, see a doctor more often, anything that could have prevented his death. She laid her palm against his cheek, loving the feel of stubble against her hand. "I should have taken better care of you."

One corner of his lips curled into a half smile. "Like I would have let you. I was stubborn, arrogant, full of bravado and the feeling of immortality. I ignored every single warning sign until it was too late. I never told you how I felt. If I had . . . oh, hell, Kate. I don't know anymore."

She brushed his hair away from his forehead, realizing how much both the boys had grown to resemble their father. "We both screwed up, Jack. We didn't take enough time to love each other. Instead, we spent our lives letting anything and everything come between us."

And then one day, he was gone. The tears flowed freely now, but she didn't care.

Jack swiped at a tear across her cheek. "I've been watching you ever since I left. This . . . I don't know what you want to call it . . . heaven, maybe? It's hard to explain, but I've been able to see you. My heart hurt watching you, baby. You had so much to live for, so much left to do with your life, and you've done nothing but wander through the city house and out here, angry at me because I left and angry at yourself because you couldn't stop it. What happened to me wasn't your fault at all. It was mine and mine alone. You need to start living again, Kate. You need to find . . ."

"Don't say it!" She pushed away from him. "Don't you dare tell me to find someone else! There is no one else but you. There never has been and there never will be! When you . . . died, my heart died too. When I married you and promised to love you forever, I goddamn well meant *forever*. 'Til death do us part doesn't mean shit to me, Jack. You are my heart, my soul, not just in this life, but in the next! So if you dare to suggest I fall in love with someone else then you don't know me at all, Jack McKay!"

He sat up and pulled her against him, stroking her hair as she finally let out all that she'd held in since the day he died. Anger fled, replaced by an abject sorrow at all they'd been denied. She sobbed, exorcising the pain that she'd forced deep inside herself for years. And through it all, Jack held her, whispering words of comfort, telling her how much he loved her and holding her tightly against him.

"Why do you think I'm here?" he finally asked. "Yes, I was supposed to encourage you to live out the rest of your years without me, but even now I'm still selfish, Katie. I don't want any man to touch you but me. I don't want you to ever love anyone else but me."

"I never will," she whispered against his chest. "I can't, Jack. I don't know how to love anyone but you." She touched his chest, wishing she could still feel the strong beat of his heart against her palm. "I don't want you to go."

"I'll never leave you, Kate. I'm here, like I've been, by your side, every single day."

He reached under the covers and pulled out a pink rose. She took it and wiped away the tears, staring in awe at the flower. To see something that could materialize out of nowhere made her truly believe in the magic. Then again, wasn't that what brought Jack back to her?

"Put this in a vase. Every day when you wake up, there'll be a fresh one in there for you."

"I'd rather have you here."

"You will. You might not see me during the day, Katie, but I'll come to you in your dreams. I can't be alive in the way you want, but we can still be together, if that's your wish."

"It is." She didn't care how, she just wanted to know that he wasn't going to leave her again.

"I won't. I'll never leave you again."

He tilted her chin up and pressed his lips against hers. She held onto his shoulders and fought the tears, instead letting her love for him well up inside her and burst forth. Passion replaced despair and she straddled his lap, kissing him deeply. Her breasts brushed his chest, her nipples aching as they scraped the fine hairs there. Jack grabbed her buttocks and rocked her against his erection, moistening the shaft with her juices.

The time for feeling sorry for herself was gone. For some unknown reason she'd been given a magical gift and she wasn't going to turn her back on a chance to love her husband for the rest of her life. No matter how it happened, whether in her dreams or some kind of alternate reality, she knew now that they would never be separated again.

It would be an unusual relationship, one that she couldn't explain to anyone, but it would be enough to know that they'd been given a second chance to be together, that the rest of her nights would be spent in the arms of the man she loved.

Lust for life renewed her and she found the strength she'd lacked for the past few years. She suddenly felt like a young girl again, her body infused with passion, eager to explore her own sexual desires and those of her man.

She dragged her pussy across his shaft, smiling when Jack let out a wild curse and dug his fingers into her hips, drawing her back and forth against his heat. She loved these moments with him. This time when they melded together as one, when she knew that all the pain she'd been through had been worth it. Loving Jack had been worth any price.

"You're going to make me crazy, Katie."

"Oh, I hope so."

He leaned back against the pillows and lifted her hips. "Ride me, baby. Fuck my cock with that sweet pussy."

Positioning his cock at her entrance, she slid down over him, leaning forward to rest her palms against his chest. She drew down on him slowly, tugging her lip with her teeth as he stretched her, filled her, his cock head striking deep. Her pussy gripped him tight and spasmed in ecstasy, her fluids pouring out and coating his cock and balls with her juices.

"So fucking hot and wet. I swear if I wasn't already dead you'd be killing me right now, Katie."

She laughed this time, no longer afraid or in pain. Rocking against him, she pleasured herself and him, splinters of fiery delight shooting straight to her core.

Jack reached for her breasts, his fingers finding her nipples and plucking them gently, adding fuel to her already consuming fire. His hands were hot, demanding, tugging, pinching, each agonizing touch against her nipples making her whimper with pleasure.

"Harder," he commanded, and she lifted, slamming down against his cock and balls, loving the way he groaned, the way his jaw tightened. "Yes, like that. Fuck me, baby."

She dragged her nails across his chest. He gasped and grabbed her wrists, pulling her chest against his and grinding his mouth against hers. He lifted his hips, powering his cock deep and hard until she felt the oncoming rush of climax.

When it hit she cried out, her moans captured by his lips as he drank in her orgasm by plunging his tongue inside her mouth. Hot jets of cream shot deep into her core as he groaned against her lips and came with her.

If she had this to look forward to the rest of her life, she'd die one very happy woman.

Drenched in sweat, they clung to each other. Kate was afraid to stop touching him, wondering when he'd disappear from her arms.

"It's not daylight yet," she whispered in his ear.

He responded by moving against her, letting her feel his shaft hardening once again. She smiled in the darkness.

It was quite possible *he* could be the death of *her*.

They made love again, all night long, each time pouring more emotion into their touches, their kisses, their whispered words to each other. The ability to give him everything made their lovemaking so much more powerful. When dawn broke, she couldn't keep her eyes open any longer. As her lids fell closed, Jack kissed her temple. "I'll always love you, Kate. I'll see you tonight."

Bright sunlight nearly blinded her. She squinted and pulled the covers over her head, but knew it was well past the time to get up.

She didn't want to get up, knowing exactly what she'd find, or not find, when she opened her eyes.

But there was no sense evading the inevitable. With a groan of protest, she threw the covers back and slid out of bed, facing the offending sun with an evil glare.

Sunlight used to be her salvation from the dreams that plagued her. Now it was her enemy and she welcomed the thought of tonight and bedtime.

A single ray of light shined on a bud vase centered on the nightstand next to her bed. In it was one pink rose.

The one Jack had given her last night. She looked around, but knew he wouldn't be there. Waiting for the inevitable despair to hit, she was surprised to feel suffused with energy and happiness. She had a million things to do before it got dark tonight.

Inspiration struck and she wrote like a woman possessed for four hours straight. The prose flowed so easily, almost as if she had been inspired.

She laughed at that. Of course she was inspired! She wrote romance! Finally, she could feel the emotions pouring through her like a life-sustaining transfusion. She was in love and she wanted to write about love, about passion, about happily ever afters. Because now she knew it was possible, that dreams really could come true. It wasn't just fairy tales and fiction. In her dreams she'd wished for Jack to come back to her, and he had.

After spending the morning writing, she showered, dressed and drove into town. The boys met her at their favorite restaurant for lunch.

"You look way too happy today," Ron said, looking more like his dad every day, all the way down to brushing that unruly thick hair off his forehead the same way Jack did.

J.J. nodded. "No kidding. You get laid last night or something?"

"J.J.!" Lord, he was just like his father, too, with his devilish grin and bawdy sense of humor. Heat suffused her cheeks. Sometimes children were far too insightful. "Actually, that isn't it at all," she lied. "I've just had a breakthrough in my book and I'm really excited about it."

"We can tell," Ron said. "Look at you. This is the liveliest I've seen you since . . ."

"Since your dad died," she finished. "It's okay. I'm not going to get angry or fall apart anymore. Life is too precious to waste." She reached for their hands. "Boys, I need to tell you something."

She took a deep breath, then expelled it. "I realize that I've spent the past five years angry at your father for dying, feeling betrayed that he hadn't lived long enough to see our dreams come true. And that wasn't right. Your father was an amazing man who made me happy from the time I was sixteen years old until the day he died."

And even after that, but she couldn't tell the boys about Jack's sudden reappearance in her life. First off, they'd never believe her and second, she knew this magical gift had to be kept between her and Jack. "But your father will never really be gone unless we forget him, and that I won't allow to happen. I don't want you to do it either. Remember him, remember his smile, the way he used to play catch and soccer with both of you when you were younger. Remember how much he loved you."

Ron pressed a hand over hers. "We knew that already, Mom. We've never forgotten Dad, or ever stopped believing in how much he loved us. It was just . . . "

She knew what he was going to say, what he didn't want to say. So she said it instead. "It was just that I was so miserably unhappy after he died that you felt guilty talking about him around me."

"Yeah," J.J. said.

"Well, that ends right now. I don't want a day to go by without talking about your Dad. We'll keep him alive by remembering his love for all of us. And I will love him with all my heart until the day I die." Fighting back tears, she smiled at her sons. "Now, you two have to make me a promise. Promise me that you will live your lives to the fullest and never take for granted how tenuous life is. We know better than most how quickly it can all be taken away from us."

They nodded, and she felt their love pouring through her. She and Jack had done a great job raising the boys. Now that the cloud of denial had been lifted, she realized what a wonderful father and husband Jack had really been. It hadn't all been bad. In fact, other than the fact he was a total workaholic, they'd had a fabulous life together.

The time for regrets was over. It was time to live again.

She thought a lot that day and well into the night as she prepared for bed. She showered, fixed her hair, sprayed on perfume and slipped on the scandalously sexy lingerie she'd bought at one of the shops today. Exhausted, she drifted off immediately.

A warm hand caressed her cheek. Something soft brushed her lips. She inhaled and caught the sweet scent of roses.

"You look hot tonight, babe."

"Jack," she sighed, welcoming him with a smile and open arms.

Epilogue

KATE FINISHED DICTATING the last chapter of her latest book, making a note for her secretary who would transcribe it in the morning. She'd long ago lost the ability to type, but she made enough money to hire a staff of people to assist her.

She smiled and shook her head, unable to believe how successful she'd become. Touted as the number one writer of romance in the world, she still managed to wow her readers even though she'd just celebrated her eightieth birthday. Her children, grandchildren and great-grandchildren had thrown her a party, and she realized while surrounded by everyone she loved what a remarkable life she'd led.

But the best part was yet to come. Dragging her worn-out body into bed, she shut out the light and waited. She was tired now. Way too tired to engage in the mad, passionate sex that she and Jack had enjoyed when he'd first returned to her.

He, of course, had never aged, while she'd grown gray and wrinkly and riddled with arthritis. He'd still come to her every night, his eyes filled with love and desire for her, despite her advanced age. To him, she was still exactly the same woman he'd fallen in love with all those years ago.

And in her dreams, she was still the same woman he'd returned to all those years ago. Still young enough to move with him when he made love to her, to feel the sparks of desire and enjoy the feel of him inside her.

She sighed, her chest aching, her old body unable to support her any longer. Her eyes drifted shut as complete exhaustion overtook her.

It didn't take long. It never did. Though tonight it was different. Instead of coming to her in the darkness, he was surrounded by a soft light that made her feel warm and comfortable.

"Katie."

He stood next to her bed and held out his hand. Surprisingly, this time it was easy to spring up and into his arms. The shackles of old age had been thrown off and she met him eagerly, their mouths meeting with passion and a love that went deeper than any words could describe.

"It's time, baby," he said, producing a pink rose. "It's your time."

She'd known that as soon as he'd come to her. That's what was different about tonight. The light was the eternal light. And she was ready. More than ready. She'd done everything she'd ever wanted to in life and it was time to be reunited with Jack.

"Now we can be together, night and day, for all eternity," he said, squeezing her in a tight hug. "No limits on our time together, no day running into night, no leaving you ever again."

What a thrill to let loose of the bounds of flesh. Joy soared within her and she felt ageless, timeless, freer than ever. The moment she'd waited years for had finally arrived. Now she stood on the same plane as the man she loved. The man she would spend forever with.

"I love you, Jack."

His eyes glistened with tears as he pressed his lips to hers. "Forever, Katie. Just as it always should have been. You and me together."

His arms enveloped hers and bright light fused them together, body, heart and soul.

Forever.

Parla's Valentine

SAMANTHA WINSTON

One

Wendy Blackmails Darla

DARLA ROODERVILLE STARED at her best friend in disbelief. "You can't be serious," she said.

"Please? I really need to go to Miami, and you're the only one I can think of who will fit in my costume!" Wendy Saks stood on Darla's porch, a bright red, sparkly sequined bikini dangling from one mittened hand and a huge, collapsible foam-rubber cake propped under her other arm. She was dressed in a large parka—it was February in upstate New York, and there were three feet of snow on the ground.

"I will not take your place as 'Queenie Lovaday.' It's out of the question. There is no way, I repeat, no way you can make me do this. Put your business on hold, go to Miami and have a great time. Call me when you get back," snapped Darla.

Darla was about to close the door, when Wendy said three words: "Your mother's diamond."

Darla froze. "You wouldn't."

"I certainly would."

"You little shit!"

"La, la, la, la, la. Poor little Darla. Borrows her mommy's wedding ring to show off and loses the diamond. Too chicken to admit it, she fills in the blank with a fake stone."

"Bitch!"

"It really doesn't matter. She'll kill you, and then, as your best friend and sole heir—I'm sure you remember our will, I'll inherit everything. I never wanted to share with you anyway," Wendy said facetiously.

"My mother wouldn't leave you the time of day." Darla was trying to keep a frown on her face, but the memory of drawing up a will with Wendy when they were kids was bringing on a serious giggle attack.

"Darla, please? Pretty, pretty, pretty please?"

"Wendy, I will not!" Darla felt her resistance slipping but she tried to sound stern.

"Look, it's easy. You set up the cake; you put on the bathing suit. You climb in the cake, you jump out of the cake yelling 'Happy Birthday, Dick Head,' or whatever you were paid to say, and you put the money in your own bank account. I'm doing you a favor and you don't even know it . . . Plus, it's a VIP client."

"How much money?" Darla asked, eyes narrowing. "You're starting to sound interesting."

"Lots." Wendy grinned.

"Why? What is so important about this client?"

"Lars Downy is organizing it."

"Okay. Lars. The guy who owns the *Daily News*." Darla shrugged. "So?"

"It's a surprise party for his best friend, Jordan Severn." Wendy raised her eyebrows.

"Who?" The name was familiar. Darla wrinkled her forehead, trying to think where she'd heard that name before.

"Hel-lo-o! Jordan? The Jordan Severn?"

Darla snapped to attention. "Wait, Jordan Severn, the Grand Hotel's new manager?"

Wendy nodded. "Yes. The Grand Hotel, owned by Tarryalot Hotels out of Boston. One of the finest hotel chains in the U.S.A." She laughed and made a face. "What I can't figure is why they decided to build one here. But who's complaining?"

"Not me," said Darla, shrugging. "Tourists mean money, and money means business."

Wendy grinned. "This town is growing by leaps and bounds," she said. "They built the Grand Hotel at the falls, and now there are not one, not two, but three gourmet shops on Main Street."

"There's always Doyle's Donuts, and don't forget T.J.'s Groceries."

"And the Cheeze Shoppe, oh, and what about Lily Haver's Hair Salon?" Wendy asked, counting on her fingers.

"Let's not leave out Phil's Gas Station and Hunting Lodge. Soon we'll be on the map," Darla said, putting considerable awe into her voice.

Wendy giggled. "We forgot Marylee's fruit and vegetable stand."

"Does it count? It's only open in the summer." Darla grinned. "We'll count it as a half a point."

"All right. And don't forget the Riverside Café, our own den of iniquity here in Harrisville." Wendy paused and her expression grew serious. "So, will you do it? Will you take my place and let me go to Miami. Please?"

"All right. You win. I'll do it. I'll jump out of your stupid cake. But only under duress and because of blackmail." Darla gave a dramatic sigh. "Come on in and have some coffee. I'm almost finished with my flower arrangements." She pointed to the old, oaken floor. "Leave your snow boots in the mud room."

"Are you doing the floral arrangements for the Grand Hotel?"

"Of course." Darla struck a pose. "I'm the only florist in town."

Wendy clapped her hand over her mouth in mock surprise. "Oh no! Did I forget to mention Smelly Buns Flower Shop?"

"Oh, very funny."

"Sorry. I meant to say Small Buds Floral Shop. Honestly Darla, couldn't you change the name?"

"It's been in the Winters family for generations. When I bought it last month, I wasn't about to insult Miss Winters by changing the name. I'll change it later."

"You're waiting for Lilac Winters to drop dead, is that it? Well, you shouldn't have long to wait. She's 104 and we're taking bets at the Riverside Café as to whether or not Ms. Winters will last the winter."

"Wendy, you really have to get some new friends." Darla shook her head in mock pity.

Wendy put on a posh English accent. "I know. That's one reason I'm going to Miami for the stripper convention. I'm hoping to find a whole new group of classy people to hang out with." She flopped onto Darla's couch.

Darla poured two cups of coffee and sat next to her. She pointed to the sequined bikini. "Now, brief me once more. I dress in this skimpy bikini, I jump out of the cake, and then I kiss the birthday boy and head out the door. Right?"

Wendy looked pained. "No! Do a little dance, sing Marilyn Monroe's rendition of 'Happy Birthday, Mr. President,' wiggle your butt a little, and let the guys stuff some bills in your bust. And *then* hit the road."

"Dance, sing, wiggle some butt and I'm outta there." Darla made a doubtful face. "I'm not really any good at singing."

"Three-thirty. Number seventy-nine Oak Street. Park across the street. Be there on time." Wendy read from a notepad she pulled from her purse. "It's all written here. Keep this. As you can see, you have Jordan's birthday party, and the next day there is a gig at the Grand Hotel." Wendy paused and peered at Darla. She must have caught the panic on Darla's face, because she patted Darla's knee and said, "Don't worry, no one will recognize you. You're just my size, and our hair is about the same. No one will look at your face when you wear this bikini. Just tell everyone you're Wendy."

Darla pouted. "Exactly how much am I getting for this? Enough to leave and make a new life elsewhere, I hope."

"Two hundred dollars a shot. If you get more business, go for it!"

"What? You think I'm going to advertise?"

"Sure! Just put a sign in the flower shop next to Miss Lilac's picture," Wendy said with a giggle.

Darla nearly choked. "I just imagined Miss Lilac jumping out of the cake." She wiped her mouth and the table with a napkin. "You should have asked her to replace you."

"No, I thought you needed some excitement in your life. Miss Lilac already has more than she can handle with her cats."

Darla looked at the cake, a frown on her face. Wendy had touched a nerve. Her life was anything but exciting. But to say that Miss Lilac had more excitement with her cats—well, that was a bit low. She plucked at a sequin.

Wendy had always wanted to be a showgirl. Darla, a nature

lover, had gotten a degree in floral decorating, then bought a flower shop in her hometown. She knew it wasn't a very glamorous life, but it was something she loved. She'd never been jealous of Wendy's life. Sure, Wendy traveled a lot, and she was always raving about her job. But Darla had never once thought of switching places.

Until today.

A little thrill of anticipation ran through her. She and Wendy had been friends since kindergarten. Wendy had always been the adventurous, crazy one. She'd always been Darla the nice, uninteresting one.

Now she was going to be Queenie Lovaday for the weekend.

Where Darla Jumps Out of a Cake

Darla arrived at Lars's house early. She parked her car across the street and set up her cake in the living room. Then she asked for somewhere she could change into her bikini. Lars showed her to his bedroom. Darla took off her clothes, folded them neatly and put them on his bed. Then she put Wendy's bikini on and looked into the full-length mirror on Lars's wardrobe.

Oh no.

She had forgotten to shave her bikini line. She clapped her hand to her forehead. She could not, would not, leap out of a cake with her fuzzy pubic hair popping out the sides of the bikini bottom. It looked like she was trying to hide a curly wig.

In Lars's bathroom, adjacent to his bedroom, was a razor and shaving cream. She got a new blade and changed it. She prayed Lars wouldn't mind her using his razor, but the situation was dire.

She locked the door, and then stepped into the shower. She spread the cream over her inner thighs and meticulously shaved them. Bending way over, she carefully shaved right up to her labia. Then, on a whim, she shaved a heart shape on her pubis. She had just finished drying herself off and was admiring her new look in the mirror, when someone banged on the door.

"Hurry up! He'll be here any second!" It was Lars.

Darla rinsed the shower and the razor, then posed in front of the mirror again. Much better. Now she looked presentable. With her shoulder-length, strawberry blond hair, lots of makeup and her curvy body shown to its utmost by the tiny bikini, she even looked hot! Her breasts were barely covered by the sequined, crocheted top. When she moved, they threatened to pop out, so she tightened the bra as much as she could.

She turned and felt her eyebrows shoot up in astonishment. A string bikini. Whoa. She'd never worn one before. Too much. She wiggled her butt.

"Hurry!" It was Lars again.

Darla hurried. She jumped into the cake and pulled the top over her head. It was dark inside the cake. As she sat there, she heard the sound of a car pulling up. Doors slammed. Then another car pulled up. Lars's voice came through the cake a bit muffled. "Hurry, come on in! Take the cars around back, Joe. Are we all here?"

A chorus of deep male voices answered. "Hey! There's the cake!" someone said.

Darla strained her ears. Who was talking? She knew almost everyone in the village. She only prayed they would think she was Wendy. She groped around the bottom of the cake for the pack of breath mints she put in there. She didn't want to sing 'Happy Birthday' while sitting on some guy's lap unless she felt cool and minty.

"You got Queenie in there?" asked one voice. "Why the cake girl, Lars?"

"It's for the man who has everything."

Someone guffawed.

"Everything but a wife," said another voice.

Lars said loudly, "Jordan can never keep a girl more than a month. I've decided he'll never get married."

"Why?"

Lars chuckled. "He's oversexed. Most girls can't take it and leave after a month."

There was an appreciative silence, then: "How long have you known him?"

Darla strained to hear. She was becoming quite interested in Jordan Severn all of a sudden.

"Since we were in college. Now be quiet, I see his car coming. Come on, let's all hide in my bedroom." Lars came over and talked to the cake. "Don't do anything until we finish singing 'Happy Birthday,' got it?"

"Yes!" Darla cried. There was a silence. The sound of a car pulling into the drive. Car doors opened and shut, and then there was a knock on the door and the sound of the front door opening. A man's voice said, "Well . . ."

"Surprise!" Lars and his friends piled out of the bedroom and started to sing. For some reason, the song faltered and stopped.

Darla bit her lip. What should she do? Lars did say to wait, but the song seemed over. In the silence, she pushed the lid off the cake, stood up and flung her arms wide, hitting someone on the face. "Happy Birthday, Dick Head!" she cried, and then choked. "I mean Jordan," she amended hastily. She gave a hasty wiggle to make her sequins sparkle, but she sensed something was not quite right.

In front of her was Jordan Severn. She'd seen him around. Who hadn't? He was, as Wendy had pointed out, the most eligible bachelor in town . . . in New York . . . in the U. S., she corrected, licking her lips. Tall, with dark brown hair, dark brown eyes and a devastating . . . scowl?

As she watched, he strode over to someone next to her and said, "Are you all right?"

Darla heard a small voice say, "She hit me."

Darla looked down to her right, and there, sitting on the couch next to the cake, was a slender young woman dressed in a navy blue suit. She was holding her gloved hands to her face. The young woman let Jordan examine her, and Darla winced. She was going to have some black eye. "I'm sorry," she said. "I didn't know anyone was standing so near. You should put some ice on that."

"You shouldn't have waved your arms like that!" snapped the woman. She glared at Darla. "Why don't you get out of that cake and out of that ridiculous costume? Jordan, I can't believe that your friends would think you'd appreciate this sort of grotesque entertainment."

"Uh, Leslie, this is Lars, Joe, Tom, Roger, Hank, Billy, and Sean. Guys, this is Leslie Tarryalot. My fiancée."

"Fiancée?" Lars's jaw dropped.

"That's right. Leslie and I are engaged." Jordan gave her a little kiss. "And this is, er, Miss Queenie Lovaday," he read, peering at the lurid red letters on the cake stand.

Leslie nodded at the group of young men, then turned her cold gaze back to Darla. "The party is over, Miss Whatever You Are. You can leave now."

Darla looked behind her. Lars and his cronies huddled in a small group. There was no help coming from that direction.

"I'm not finished yet," said Darla, gathering her courage. "I still have to sing a song to the birthday boy." She did an impromptu belly dance, and was rewarded by a definite lift of Jordan's eyebrows. She leaned over, to give him a good view of her cleavage, and sang in a breathy voice, "Happy—"

"I said, it's time to go!" said Leslie, standing up now. Jordan stood too, and offered his hand to Darla.

"I think it's better you leave. Here, let me help you."

Darla smiled at him gratefully. She lifted one leg out of the cake . . .

. . . and tripped. She plunged forward, and Jordan made a grab at her. His hands met her breasts with a loud slap. She shrieked, flung her arms around his waist, and they crashed to the floor. Jordan on his back, Darla lying on him, her face pressed to his. His hands were still on her breasts. Both hands, cupping her breasts. She couldn't think why for a second, then she realized that in the fall, he'd accidentally slipped his hands beneath her tight bikini top, and now they were stuck.

She wriggled her hips, trying to roll off him. What happened next was his belt caught on her crocheted sequined bikini bottom. Their foreheads were still pressed together, but now they were getting rather warm. Darla thought that her whole body must be scarlet. Waves of heat were washing through her.

"Excuse me," Darla said to Jordan, her lips brushing his.

He seemed incapable of movement. But one of his hands tightened on her breast. The effect was immediate and intense. Darla felt a rush of heat between her thighs. It had been far too long since she'd been with a man. She gave a little moan.

"I think we're stuck," said Jordan. His voice sounded odd.

"Do something!" shrieked Leslie.

"Don't move!" cried Darla, "you'll tear my bikini!" She writhed a bit more, trying to release herself, and felt a definite change in Jordan's anatomy. That which had been soft, grew hard.

"Get off of him, you slut!" Leslie screamed.

"How dare you!" Darla heaved upwards. Her bikini top popped off. Her breasts were still covered by Jordan's hands, and she could feel her nipples tingling and hardening.

"Don't let go," she said to him under her breath. His hands tightened. Oh my god. She resisted the urge to rub her crotch against Jordan's.

For a second she resisted.

What harm could it do? It was going to be quick, that was sure. She was on the brink of a very explosive orgasm. She'd never been so turned on.

She ground her hips into his, and was rewarded when his belt pressed into her clit. She opened her legs wide and arched her back, pressing, and pressing, *Oh God! Yes!* She came in a starburst of throbbing. Her nipples hardened in Jordan's palms. She could feel them lengthening. His hands tightened again. *Oh God.*

Was it possible to be more embarrassed? Sweat trickled off her forehead, down her cheek and landed on Jordan's lips. Yes, she supposed, there was always room for more humiliation. "Sorry," she whispered.

"Please," he gasped. Please what? Get off? Rub some more? His penis was rock hard against her inner thighs.

"Get off him!" wailed Leslie.

Panting, Darla reached down and fumbled at his belt to release her bikini. Instead, she released the buttons on his fly, and his huge erection—because that's what it was at this point—sprang out between her thighs. She gave a little squeak, and clamped her thighs together, intending to hide it from view. Legs together, she could feel his cock throbbing. She squeezed tighter, and reached down to close his pants.

Someone pulled at her shoulder.

"Wait!" she said.

It was too late. Leslie screamed and made another grab for Darla. "Get off of him, you tramp!" She yanked Darla backwards, and Darla sat down hard on her butt, baring Jordan's astounding anatomical attribute.

Jordan grabbed at his penis, and managed to stuff it back in his pants. Darla felt a definite pang of regret.

"You wanton bitch!" Leslie hissed, and she hit Darla on the head with her purse and stormed out of the house. From outside came the sound of tires squealing.

"Would you please get out of here?" Darla cried at the group of men, still huddled near the bedroom door. In two seconds flat, they were gone, except for Lars and Jordan. Lars held out a towel.

Darla grabbed it, held it to her chest, squashed her cake flat with one foot, and ran into Lars's bedroom and locked his door. She put on her clothes, and then opened his window. Thank goodness it was on the ground floor. She tossed the cake out, and then jumped into a large snowdrift. She dashed across the street to her car and flung the cake into the back seat. For a second she stood there, a bit stunned, then she leapt into the car and drove back to her cottage.

Belatedly, she remembered she'd forgotten to unlock Lars's bedroom door.

Lars poured a large glass of scotch and handed it to Jordan. "Here, you look like you could use this."

"Thanks." Jordan sipped at the fiery liquid and sighed as it warmed his throat and stomach.

"Should you go after, um, what was your fiancée's name again?"

"Leslie." Jordan winced. "I think I'll give her a while to cool off. I'm sure she'll understand." He tried to make his voice sound more positive than he felt. What a fiasco!

Lars nodded. "A wise decision."

"What made you hire a cake-girl?"

"Queenie? I, er, thought it was a good idea—at the time. I'm sorry Jordan, I had no idea you were engaged. This is very sudden, isn't it?"

"We're not technically engaged," Jordan said. Lars looked upset, but it wasn't his fault. Jordan gave him a reassuring grin. "Look, don't feel bad. I'm sure Leslie will forget all about this."

"When did you meet?"

"Actually, I've known her for a while. Her father owns Tarryalot Hotels, and I've been working for him for five years now. Leslie and I ran into each other a few times, and last month we started dating."

"And?" Lars raised his eyebrows. "She's hot in the sack?"

Jordan choked on his whiskey. "We haven't slept together yet."

Now it was Lars's turn to sputter. "What? You mean that you haven't made love to her yet?" he sputtered. "What happened to the Jordan I knew in college? Mr. Screw-all-night-and-day?"

Jordan drained his glass and held it out. "More."

"Well?" Lars poured him a glassful. "What happened?"

"I woke up," said Jordan. "I realized that sex wasn't everything in a relationship."

Lars tossed the rest of his drink back and raised one eyebrow. "Oh? And how did you come to that conclusion?"

"After much heartache and thought," said Jordan, a spark of anger in his voice. He was surprised to hear it, and he wondered if he were getting drunk. "What business is it of yours anyway?"

"Hey! I'm on your side, remember?" Lars peered at his glass. "More?"

"No, I'll get sloshed, and I have to go apologize to Leslie." Jordan sighed. He was not looking forward to Leslie's forthcoming tantrum. Changing the topic to something more pleasant, he asked, "Who was that cake girl anyway?"

Lars beamed. "Queenie Lovaday. Isn't she hot?" His grin broadened. "I couldn't help noticing that you seemed to appreciate her, um, charms."

Queenie Lovaday. What a ridiculous name for such a hot chick. Just thinking about her got him hard, though. Jordan tipped his head back and groaned. "I haven't had a boner like that since college. I still ache."

"Well, look on the bright side. Now Leslie knows exactly what she's getting."

"Oh, very funny."

"Come on, Jordan. I'll drive you back to the hotel, and I'll help you explain everything to your fiancée. Just let me get my keys."

"Where are they?"

"In my bedroom."

Once back home, Darla inspected the damage to Wendy's bikini. It was minimal, nothing she couldn't fix.

Too bad she couldn't fix the party. What a disaster! She'd jumped out of the cake, called him Dick Head, given his fiancée a black eye and practically raped him right before her eyes.

She gave a frustrated sigh. There was no way she was going to get paid for today's ignominy. The four hundred badly needed dollars was now halved. Oh well. There was always tomorrow's gig, Darla told herself.

She made herself dinner and sat in her bed, watching TV. At least, that's what she was trying to do. But her mind kept straying back to the moment when she rubbed up against Jordan Severn's cock. Her pussy throbbed in delight.

Darla reached under the covers and grabbed herself. "None of that now," she scolded. It was too late. Just the thought of Jordan was making her hot.

"Oh no," she groaned.

She hadn't had a boyfriend since college. And Stan had been such a disaster, she wasn't looking forward to another relationship. The problem was she was too demanding. Stan had made that perfectly clear. She wanted to make love once or twice a day. He was a twice a week man, and that was including once on weekends. Darla got hot just thinking of cock. Just thinking about it made her pussy swell and juices run down her thigh. Like now.

She flipped over in bed and rubbed her breasts against the pillow. "If only you were Jordan," she breathed. "No, I take that back. He's engaged and I made a vow never to flirt with married men. Engaged is as good as married. If only you were someone who looked like Jordan with a big, strong, hard cock like he has," she said. She rolled over and humped the pillow, but of course its anatomy left a lot to be desired.

Darla sat up, her face flushed, her hair tangled. She looked down at her pussy. Its new heart-shaped haircut suited it. She spread her legs and touched it. It was slick and swollen, and as soon as her finger brushed against her clit she nearly came all over her hand. "All right. You win."

She reached into her drawer and took out her Eden's Fall Special, a red, white and blue sparkly vibrator. Darla liked it. Too bad it wasn't attached to a hot and heavy male body.

She pushed the button and stroked her clit. Just thinking about Jordan was wreaking havoc with her libido. Damn him anyway—he was engaged. If he knew she was fantasizing about him, he'd probably . . . spank her. She imagined him putting her over his knees and then spreading her thighs with one hand while he gave her a little spanking with the other.

"Oh yes, Jordan, hit me harder!" She could almost feel his hand coming down on her buttocks. The imaginary slap stung, and the tingle went straight to her belly. She pictured him bending over her, holding her thighs firmly with one hand, while he spanked her teasingly with the other. Not hard enough to hurt, but hard enough to sting and to make her wet with excitement. Afterwards, he'd gently stroke the pink marks, rubbing his hand over the smooth curve of her ass, maybe tickling a little as he leaned down to kiss her. His breath would be hot on the sensitive skin of her buttocks. His tongue would dart out and he'd lick her, starting at the back of her thigh, easing into the crack between her legs, parting them with his hands, and then slowly penetrating her aching cunt with his tongue and fingers, while she writhed on his lap, her legs spread wide.

Lying on her back, she lifted her hips and slammed the vibrator into her cunt. She put her pillow on top of her, feeling her nipples rubbing against the smooth cotton. She clutched at the vibrator, and in her mind she pictured a man who looked like Jordan with his magnificent cock. She teetered on the brink of orgasm, then, with one last cry, she wrapped her legs around her pillow and thrust the vibrator up as far as it would go.

It filled her, not as much as Jordan's cock would, but enough. Her hips jerked in tempo to her hands as she started to come. Her cunt throbbed, pulsed, contracted around the vibrator and Darla uttered a shrill cry. "Jordan!"

Three

When the Elevator Gets Stuck

THE NEXT DAY, wearing her mended bikini under her long, winter coat, collapsible foam-rubber cake in tow, Darla rushed into the elevator at the Grand Hotel. She was late! Her car had broken down, the tow truck had gotten a flat tire, and her "show" was in three minutes on the seventh floor. She'd had to change into her costume at the garage, and now she was about frozen. She just barely squeezed into the elevator before the door slid closed.

She uttered a huge sigh, dropped the cake, turned and screamed, "You!"

Jordan Severn backed into the corner and stared at her. His eyes took in the trench coat and the cake. "You again," he breathed.

"I'm so sorry about yesterday, Jordan!" Darla cried. She could feel her cheeks turning bright red. Her body misinterpreted her words. It seemed to think that the word "Jordan" meant "orgasm." As soon as his name left her lips, she felt a strong twinge in her pussy. It grew into a throbbing as she stood there, trying to look cool and collected. It didn't help that the string bikini touched her in all the right places. It dug right into her ass and rubbed hard.

185

Her pussy swelled, she could feel her labia getting bigger and her crotch started getting wet. She tried not to wiggle as her nipples began to tingle.

"That's all right. Lars straightened it out with Leslie. He explained everything. It's as much my fault as it is yours. I, er, hadn't been with a woman in a long time. It was a bit overwhelming for me." He blushed, deeply, and Darla stared in fascination. She'd never seen a man blush.

"Same here," she said. "I mean, not with a woman. I meant, I haven't done anything with a man for ages and . . . Please, why can't I just shut up?" She pressed her legs together beneath her coat. Her pussy was clenching and unclenching like a fist. Her juices were starting to leak onto her thigh. Her bikini was going to be soaked—the evidence of her wanton desire was going to be hard to hide when she jumped out of the cake.

"It's a rather delicate situation. We've only known each other for a few weeks. Her father is my boss," explained Jordan.

"I thought you were engaged." Darla tried to concentrate on their conversation, determined to calm her depravity.

"Our engagement party is set for tomorrow night."

"Congratulations," Darla said then winced. It didn't sound like she meant it at all. Well, if she were honest with herself, she had to admit that she was disappointed.

He shrugged. "Thank you."

The elevator shuddered and stopped. The door did not open.

"Now what?" Jordan muttered.

"We're stuck." Darla punched the alarm. Nothing happened. She pushed the floor buttons. Nothing happened.

"Here, let me try this." Jordan picked up the intercom and spoke into it. "Hello, we're stuck! Can anyone hear us?"

A minute later, a voice crackled on the line. "Don't worry. In ten minutes we'll have it fixed. It's nothing."

"Great. I'm going to be late," Darla sighed. "Where are you going?"

"Sixth floor. My fiancée is waiting, probably right at the elevator door. She hates it when I'm late."

Darla gulped. "If she sees me here, you'll probably get fired and the engagement will be called off. Look, I know how I can make it up to you." She glanced at the ceiling. The talk about his fiancée put a bit of a damper on her traitorous pussy. She felt a bit calmer now. "Boost me up and I'll quickly go out the door just above us."

"Can you do that?"

"Sure, I've done it before," lied Darla. Well, she'd seen it done in films. "If the door is open a crack, I can just push it open and Leslie will never know I'm here."

"Tell me if the door is open." Jordan leaned down, and Darla shrugged off her winter coat.

"My God!" Jordan exclaimed. "Where are your clothes?"

"I'm late, I had to change in the garage," she explained.

"Aren't you cold?" His eyes were glued to her tits. In response, her tits obligingly tingled, and her nipples hardened so quickly that one pushed right out of the crochet. She could feel it. She didn't dare look down.

"I'm kind of hot, actually," she said. Her breasts were now aching so much she could hardly think. She was afraid that in a second she would start begging him to suck them.

She kicked off her boots and climbed on his shoulders then, pushing the trap door open, stood up on his shoulders. She could just reach the bottom of the door, but when she tried to pry it open, it wouldn't budge. What was worse, just the feel of Jordan's hands on her legs keeping her upright, was making her so horny she was practically cross-eyed. "It's tightly closed. Damn. Sorry about that. Hold on, I'm coming down." She put one knee on his shoulder, trying to keep her very damp, very aroused pussy away from his face.

At that moment, the elevator jolted and started moving. Jordan lost his balance and fell backwards, luckily landing on the soft, foam rubber cake. Darla grabbed at the ceiling, but it was too late. She landed on her knees, her head snapped forward and she hit the wall. Stunned, she sat down hard, her crotch pressed against Jordan's chin. The elevator door opened.

"Oh my God!"

Darla turned around, half dazed. Leslie stared back at her. "You!" they cried at the same moment.

Darla's head was still ringing, so it took her a minute to figure out why Leslie was screeching. She looked down. All she saw was the top of Jordan's head. His face was wedged firmly between her thighs. His breath was hot, and right on her cunt. The string was no barrier. His mouth moved, and tickled her labia. They were so swollen they'd escaped both sides of the tiny bikini and now were hugging it tightly. The crocheted bikini crotch was shoved against her clit and wedged into her vagina. Or was that Jordan's chin?

There must not be much space between his lips and hers. She felt another rush of heat between her legs. His hands came up and groped for her, meeting her naked backside. That did it. She started to come. It was a mini-orgasm, but very intense. She pressed her pulsing cunt against his mouth. Her whole body shuddered violently as waves of electricity shot through her.

"Get off of him, you bitch!" Leslie looked horrified. "What on earth do you think you are doing?"

Darla managed to stagger to her feet. Jordan sat up and handed her the cake. He was rather red-faced and didn't look her in the eye. When she glanced at his crotch, she saw why. There was a large, telltale bulge there. She grabbed the cake. He looked at her then, and she felt her breath leave her lungs in a whoosh. Damn it! Why did he have to be so sexy? Why did he have to have those smoldering eyes and that . . .

"Get out of here, you bitch!"

. . . And that irritating fiancée? "I'm leaving," Darla muttered.

"Here you . . . hey, wait a minute, you hurt yourself!" Jordan cried.

Darla wasn't waiting for anything. She snatched up coat and boots, and fled. She pushed past Leslie and managed to find the stairs where she hid for a few minutes, trembling, the cake clutched to her chest. Then she put on her coat and boots, made her way to the parking lot where her rent-a-car was parked. She was dizzy, and had a bit of a time finding the ignition. When the car finally started she drove carefully home.

Her head was still hurting. When she looked in the mirror, she saw a huge lumpy bruise on her forehead. She touched it gingerly. Damn. She looked awful. And she was frozen. No wonder—running around in a bikini in February. With a sigh, she got an icepack and held it to her head. She swallowed a couple aspirin and crawled into her bed.

She'd blown her entire weekend. Not one disaster but two. Not a cent in her bank account, and although she never would have admitted it to Wendy, she was desperate for cash. She'd bought her house five years ago, but the flower shop was a recent purchase, and the bank nearly hadn't approved the loan. If she was late with just one payment, they were going to come down hard on her.

Just then her business phone rang. She frowned at it. It was Sunday. Didn't these people ever take a break? She'd transferred her number to her cell phone, she remembered belatedly, and forgotten to transfer it back to the shop. "Yes?"

"Hello, Miss Winter's Small Buds Flower Shop? This is Jordan Severn. I'm sorry to call on a weekend, but something came up, and you're the only flower shop in the area."

"How can I help you, Mr. Severn?" croaked Darla. She realized, with a rush of relief, that he had no idea who she really was. She decided to impersonate Lilac Winters. Thank goodness she hadn't had time to change the shop name or telephone listing.

"Well, Miss Winters, I'm giving an engagement party for my fiancée and our parents at the Grand Hotel tomorrow night." He gave a slight cough. "I, er, need a lot of flowers. Actually, I also need a big bouquet right now, if it's possible."

"A big bouquet?"

"With lots of red roses, and a card saying, 'Forgive me.'"

"Forgive you?" Darla raised her eyebrows. "For what? It wasn't your fault. I mean, I'm sure it wasn't your fault, whatever it was. You sound like such a charming young man," she babbled.

"Well . . . " Jordan sounded mystified. "It wasn't actually my fault. I keep running into this nutty woman."

"Nutty woman?" Darla dug her nails into her palm. How embarrassing. He thought she was a nut! "So, what shall I put on the card? 'Forgive me, I keep running into a nut?'"

"No, no! I didn't say that."

"Well, if you'll excuse me for saying, just 'Forgive me' is pretty lame."

Darla's Valentine

"Ma'am?"

Darla chewed thoughtfully on her lower lip. She wanted to know exactly what Jordan thought of her. She wasn't content with being a nut. Maybe she could draw him out a bit. "You have to explain why you want her to forgive you. Take it from me. I'm an old woman with lots of experience in this matter. In matters of the heart," she amended.

"You're right, of course. Just put, 'For my darling Leslie, I know I can count on your understanding. It was a silly accident. She was trying to go for help and we fell. I'm sorry you took it the wrong way.' No, I mean, 'I'm sorry I hurt your feelings.' Sign it 'Love, Jordan.' Um, do you think that will do?"

Darla lay back on her bed. She pressed the cell phone closer to her ear. Her other hand crept under her panties. Just the sound of his voice was making her wet. "Tell me exactly what happened, and why your fiancée is so angry," she said. "I'll tell you if that will do." She slid a finger into her cunt.

Jordan cleared his throat. "Well, it was the strangest thing. Yesterday was my birthday, and my best friend decided to hire a stripper."

"A what?" Darla's hand stopped its gentle, in and out movements. "A stripper?"

"Well, not exactly. A scantily dressed woman to jump out of a rubber cake. She was cute."

"Cute? Only cute?"

Jordan hesitated. "She was very sexy, actually. Anyhow, to tell the truth, I didn't really see her face. I was, um, looking at her bosom."

"Her bosom. Young man, you stared at another woman's bosom in front of your fiancée? You looked at another woman's breasts?" Darla twisted her finger around in her slippery cunt and rubbed

191

her thumb against her clit. She was so wet! Her hand was making sucking noises as she thrust in and out. "Did you . . . did you like it?" she managed to ask.

"Um, unfortunately, I did. Then she fell on me, and we got tangled up and her bikini got stuck on my fly and my hands were, well . . ."

"Where were your hands, young man?" She made her voice stern like a school teacher and hoped that would encourage him to confess.

"Inside her bikini top. They were right on her breasts."

"Oh, my! So, she was lying on top of you, is that it? And you were underneath her?"

"That's right. And then she started wiggling to get loose, and it made everything worse, because it's been so long since I've . . ." Jordan stopped.

"No, please, go on," Darla panted. She thrust two fingers deep into her hot pussy and thrummed her clit, hard. It vibrated like a guitar string. She uttered a soft moan.

"Are you all right, ma'am?"

"Yes!" Darla cried, humping her hips against her hand. "Please, tell me more. Go on. She was on top of you, and then?"

"It's rather embarrassing to speak of it," said Jordan stiffly.

"Speak!"

"Well, I'm a young man, and well, my body reacted rather, um, strongly to her. It's been a while since I've been with a woman, you see."

"I'm of an age where nothing shocks me anymore," said Darla, reaching to her drawer and groping around for her Eden's Fall Special. She pulled too hard and the drawer fell to the floor with a loud crash.

"Are you all right?"

"Yes, of course. You were saying, young man? Your body reacted?" Frantically, she groped along the floor. She grabbed her vibrator, ripped off her underwear and shoved it into her pussy. It felt odd and there was a strong buzzing in her ear. Then she realized, she was listening to her vibrator.

Cursing, she switched in time to hear Jordan say, " . . . and then she reached between my legs to try to unhook her bikini."

Her phone was covered in her juices; her musk filled her nostrils. She pumped her vibrator between her legs, feeling it sliding into her quivering vagina, stretching her tender flesh. It had been too long since she'd been with a man. If only this was attached to a real person. To a big, thick, energetic cock on someone like Jordan. Why couldn't she stop thinking about him? Was it his good looks? The sense of humor that sparkled in his eyes? His . . . "Oh God," she gasped.

"You guessed it." Jordan gave an embarrassed laugh. "I couldn't control myself. It was the strangest thing that ever happened to me. And the worst thing is, I'm sure the young lady felt the same way. I could feel her . . ."

"Feel her?"

"She was as excited as I was. I could tell."

"How?"

"Er, her nipples were hard and she was moving her hips, you know . . . and well, I could just tell, that's all." He cleared his throat.

"And today?" Somehow Darla managed to control her voice as she pushed the vibrator in and out of her swollen cunt. She was so hot! His voice was so seductive, she had a mini-orgasm every time he opened his mouth. And thinking of his mouth, open, pressed against her breasts . . . *No! Stop it Darla!* she thought furiously. *Think of someone else! Think of some hunky movie star with his hard cock pounding into your slippery, slick, quivering flesh. Oh Yes! Wait, what is he saying now?* She paused, the vibrator sheathed fully within her pussy.

"I ran into her again, and we were in the elevator when it got stuck. I honestly didn't mean for anything to happen, but when she climbed on my shoulders, and I looked up, I got so hard I let go of her and we fell."

"Didn't the elevator start with a jerk?"

"Huh? How did you know?"

"I guessed. Just a guess. Looking upwards wouldn't make you both fall." Darla withdrew the vibrator and held it lightly against her clit. She gasped as it tickled her sensitive nub. When they'd fallen, his mouth had been pressed to her clit and she'd felt his lips moving against her own labial lips. She drew the vibrator across her labia, pressing them apart then squeezing them together. They were so sensitive now that she only had to touch them softly and they clamped together in delight. If only Jordan . . . *Flowers she had to think of flowers. Anything but the thought of sitting on Jordan's . . .*

"Well, we fell and she landed on my face. It was . . . well, I could feel her, and she rubbed herself on me, and I just got excited again." His voice cracked. "Talking about it is, well, difficult." He paused and then said ruefully, "Anyway, that's when the elevator door opened."

Darla couldn't hold it off another second. She dug her heels into her bed and raised her hips to the sky, plunging the vibrator deep into her cunt, pumping madly. "Yes, yes, yes!" she cried before exploding into a mind-blowing orgasm. From her head to her toes, her whole body vibrated. Her vision went black for a second as her insides convulsed.

"Ma'am? Ma'am are you all right?" He sounded concerned.

"Fine, I'm fine. Just a little heat stroke, that's all." She could hardly breathe. Panting, she fanned herself with her hand, her cunt still twitching with paroxysms of lust.

"Heat stroke? It's February." His voice rose in disbelief.

Darla blinked, gathering her thoughts. Embarrassment was the first thing that flitted through her head. Then she sighed in relief. He thought she was an old lady. He didn't suspect anything. "Don't worry. I'll have the flowers delivered to the Grand Hotel in an hour."

"What about tomorrow night? I need at least fifteen bouquets. I want to decorate my entire suite. I have to make a good impression." He said that firmly.

"Impression?"

"Er, yes. Leslie's parents and my parents are coming for the engagement, and I'm having a private dinner party in my suite. Since Leslie's father is my boss, I want to make a good impression," he explained.

"You will. What time should I deliver them?"

He was all business now, Queenie and her effect on him shoved completely aside, it seemed. "Well, everyone is coming at seven, so be there at six. I'll have the concierge let you in and you can decorate the suite with flowers."

"Very well, young sir." Darla clicked off and gave her cell phone a lick. "Well, if I ever lose my Eden Special, I know what to do," she said. "I can set it for vibrating mode, and call myself with my home phone line."

A huge yawn nearly dislocated her jaw. She sat up and spoke to herself sternly. "Don't go to sleep. I have to make a bouquet for Miss Leslie Tarryalot."

Sighing, she turned and buried her head in her pillow. "I'm nothing but an oversexed jezebel," she moaned. "Why can't I find a boyfriend? I don't want casual sex! I want a husband who loves me and will screw me every night! Damn it, is that too much to ask for?"

She looked at the ceiling. "It's Valentine's Day tomorrow, and no one has ever deserved a Valentine more than I do. I've been good; I've been waiting for Mr. Right, and all I got was Stan. I dumped Stan, so now I have no one. I don't date married men and I refuse to screw up Jordan's life. So, please, St. Valentine hear my plea. Send me a Valentine. Any nice, stiff cock will do as long as it's attached to a kind, loving man who will adore me for the rest of my life."

Darla looked and found she was praying with her vibrator clasped to her heart. "I'm hopeless," she groaned.

She dressed, drove to town. It was Sunday and she hadn't been planning on working, so she hadn't brought any flowers home. Her flower shop was on Main Street, and still had Lilac Winter's portrait in the window. Darla made up a whimsical, romantic bouquet using red roses, curly green fern, and white tuberose. Rubbing her eyes, trying to stay awake, she attached a handwritten note and dropped it off at the Grand Hotel.

four

Jordan Gets to Know Leslie Better

"Who the hell is Darla?"

Jordan grabbed the note and stared at it. "I have no idea. I called Ms. Winter's shop and—"

"Ms. Winter?" It was Lars. He had come to the hotel to have dinner with Jordan and Leslie. Leslie had stormed into the dining room like a Valkyrie, shrieking something about a Darla.

"You know Ms. Winter?" Jordan asked, praying for a distraction.

"She's a hundred and four. At least. She must have misunderstood or forgotten. Poor old dear."

"She must have meant to write 'Darling'," said Jordan, pulling Leslie's chair out, and giving her a placating smile. "Have a seat." He wondered why Leslie was sounding so shrill. Couldn't she relax? "It was a simple mistake. An old lady meant to write 'Darling' and it came out 'Darla,' that's all," he said to her, his tone soothing.

Leslie calmed down after that. "Well, the flowers were beautiful. Thank you, Jordan."

Lars patted her hand. "So, how do you like this part of the woods?" he asked.

"It's very . . . wild," Leslie said with a sniff.

"Tourists appreciate the natural beauty of the setting," agreed Lars. "Nothing but forest and lakes and rivers. There are deer and bear in the woods, and there are some incredible nature walks and hiking trails. Would you like to go on a snowshoe trail? We can fix you up with . . ."

"No, thank you. I'm not a very outdoorsy sort of person." Leslie looked at the menu. "It will be nice for a season, but I'm looking forward to going back to Boston."

"Just a season? You want to live in Boston?" Jordan frowned. "We'll be here for many years, I hope." He plucked restlessly at his napkin. Living in the backwoods had always been his aspiration. He wanted Leslie to love it here as much as he did.

"I'm sure Daddy will promote you as soon as we're married and we can move back to civilization." Leslie rolled her eyes. "You can't really imagine me living here, can you?"

Jordan wasn't sure what to imagine. He'd been enchanted with the town and the immense wilderness all around. This hotel had been his dream. "We'll see," he said, hoping she'd come around to his way of thinking.

Leslie motioned for a waiter. "Can we order please?" she asked, then looked at Jordan. "I can't wait for our engagement party. Have you organized everything?"

Jordan nodded. "It's all set, from the dinner to the flowers." At least he hoped it was all set. Could he trust old Miss Lilac not to screw things up?

He decided not to worry about it. Leslie and her family would just have to take him as he was.

"Perfect," said Leslie.

When the waiter arrived, she said, "I'll have the smoked salmon to start, and afterwards the filet mignon, well done."

Jordan watched her. The candlelight softened her expression and made her pale hair glow. But for some reason, the vision of another woman kept superimposing itself over her features—someone smaller, rounder, and with mischievous brown eyes fringed in long, black lashes. Someone with strawberry blond hair and lovely, round, firm breasts. Beneath the table, his penis grew hard and he shifted uncomfortably.

If only Leslie would let him make love to her. But she wouldn't even let him feel her breasts. She informed him that she was a virgin, and intended to stay that way until her wedding night.

Fine. He admired that and respected her wishes. But he was young, healthy, and horny most of the time. His former girlfriends had all told him he was oversexed, and that he should try cold showers more often. He didn't know about that. All he knew was, if he didn't get some pussy, and soon, he was going to explode. He wondered what date Leslie would choose for their wedding. Sometime very soon, he hoped.

He looked at Leslie and tried to imagine her naked. For some reason, his penis deflated. Odd. He closed his eyes and tried again.

"Are you all right?" Leslie asked.

"A bit tired," Jordan admitted.

Lars raised his eyebrows. "You better get to bed early. You have a long day tomorrow."

After dinner, Leslie accompanied him to his suite. She'd had a few glasses of wine, surreptitiously topped up by a grinning Lars, and she was in a good mood, for once. When he drew her into his arms and kissed her, she didn't draw back. Instead, she opened her mouth and gave him a passionate kiss.

Her arms tightened, and she started to rub her belly against his. Hardly believing his luck, he slid his hands beneath her dress and rubbed his hand lightly between her legs. She was wearing stockings and underwear. He didn't try to bypass them, but she opened her legs and pressed harder against his hand. He rubbed some more, and then unbuttoned her blouse and exposed her bra.

Still with one hand between her legs, he slid her bra strap off and bared a pale breast. Her nipple was small and pink. He leaned down and sucked on it, flicking the nipple with his tongue. It stayed soft, but she arched her back and made a kind of moaning sound. Panting, he massaged her breast, wondering if she'd let him take her underwear off.

She drew back and looked at him. "Show me your manhood," she whispered.

Manhood?

"All right." He fumbled with his belt, and then unbuttoned his fly. She pushed his pants down and he stood in front of her. Her blouse was half off, and her hair disheveled. He should have been erect. But apparently, his penis was not in the mood. How odd.

Leslie saw his expression and said, "Don't worry, I can help. I've been thinking . . . seeing you with that trampy girl made me realize that you had needs that I should take care of."

"You should? You can? I thought you were a virgin."

"I am. That doesn't mean I've never sucked a man's penis."

That bit of information threw him. It didn't fit the Leslie he thought he knew. "Oh? Whose was that?" he asked.

"I tried it once in my senior year."

"In high school?"

"No. Honestly Jordan. In college. Do you have a condom?"

"Er . . . Yes." He fumbled in his wallet and found a rubber. He wondered why she wanted one. "Um, do you think a rubber is necessary?" he asked delicately.

She looked up at him, and said, "Jordan Severn, I really don't think I have to explain anything. But if you really have to know, I just finished a wonderful dinner and I don't want anything to spoil it."

Jordan wondered what she meant by that, but then decided he didn't want to ask. He would try to enjoy this the best he could and have a long talk with her afterwards. When she was in a good mood. Whenever that would be.

Leslie knelt in front of him, after taking a cushion off the couch and putting it on the ground. Then she pulled her hair back and twisted it into a bun. She drew a deep breath, and touched his penis. She pulled at it with her fingertips, and then pumped it in her hand. She took the rubber out of the packet and tried to slide it on his unresponsive cock.

No luck. His penis slid right out. She wasn't one to give up though. Lips tight, a frown on her face, Leslie finally managed to squash it in somewhat, holding the rubber and pushing his penis with her thumbs.

Jordan watched, horrified and fascinated at the same time. He didn't know if he should be embarrassed or start to laugh. Leslie gave another shove to his penis, and it disappeared into the rubber. Jordan wondered if it had gone into hiding. He wished he could disappear into something small right about now.

"Voilà," she said, triumphantly.

Jordan raised his eyebrows. *Voilà what?*

Leslie leaned over, kissed his crumpled, rubberized penis, slid her lips quickly over it, and pushed her breasts against his thighs.

Then she frowned and looked up at him. "What's the matter?"

Jordan had no idea. He was as soft as ever. He felt his cheeks flaming. "I think I drank too much and I'm tired."

"That must be it." She stood up, put her clothes back in order and straightened her hair. She pecked him on the lips. "Well, tomorrow is another day." She looked relieved, he thought.

"Good night," said Jordan. He had a sick feeling in the pit of his stomach.

What on earth was happening to him? One minute he was fantasizing about a hot little stripper, and the next . . . oh, oh. His cock was rising. He stared at it. "Queenie Lovaday?" he said to it.

His cock thickened. The rubber dropped off the end and fell on the floor with a little plop.

"Leslie?"

His penis shrunk.

"Queenie?"

It hardened.

He pictured Queenie standing in front of him in her ridiculously skimpy bikini. As he watched, she reached up and unfastened the top. Two, round breasts popped out, with hard nipples pointing right at him.

He looked at his penis. It stood at attention, quivering, ready to go.

Or to come.

He moaned and took it in his hands. In his mind, he saw the wide, smiling mouth of Queenie Lovaday open and slide over his cock's tip. He pictured his penis disappearing into her mouth, and he slid his hand back and forth. His hand was her lips. He imagined her kneeling in front of him, her sexy mouth open, her smooth tongue darting out and touching the tip of his penis.

A wave of heat washed over him. Suddenly he was spurting all over his hands. His cum shot out so fast all he could do was clutch at his twitching cock as if it were a thrashing trout he'd just caught at the river.

"Good grief," he said, staring at his damp hands and the spots of cum on the rug. He looked up at the ceiling, half convinced he'd see cum up there too. "What am I going to do?" he asked.

five

The Dinner Party From Hell

"IT'S FOUR A.M. already, I have to hurry. Roses, check. Baby's breath, check. Yellow mimosa, check. Sweetpea, check. Ferns, check. Violets, check." Darla rubbed her forehead and went over the list again. She needed more flowers. With a sigh, she realized she'd have to make a run to Montreal. It would take her four hours, there and back, but she needed fresh flowers. This was her chance to redeem herself.

She felt like a dreadful slut fantasizing about another woman's fiancée. It just wasn't like her. She and Wendy had made a vow while in high-school never to flirt with a married man. She'd never broken it, and she never would. Instead, she would make the most beautiful, romantic floral decoration the world had ever seen.

She made herself a thermos of coffee, pulled on her parka and her boots, and went outside to scrape off the snow on her car. It had snowed during the night, and the world sparkled and glittered beneath the full moon. Humming along with the song on the radio, she turned the heater on full blast, and set off through the sleeping countryside, following the tracks left by the snowplows.

Once on the highway, the going was better. The sun rose as she crossed the Saint Lawrence River, and she admired the pink and golden splendor of the new day.

"Happy Valentine's day!" proclaimed the banner strung up over the entrance to the market in Montreal. "Oh yeah, right," Darla muttered as she pulled her trolley along, picking out flowers. She gazed at a display of waxy, pink tulips and exuberant, scarlet peonies. Her mouth trembled. Wouldn't it be nice to receive a bouquet of flowers for once, instead of always making them for others?

She returned with a trunk full of fragrant flowers and spent the day at the shop, alternately serving clients and working on the decorations for Jordan's dinner. Soon the backroom was full of garlands, posies and bouquets. Darla ties swaths of ivy together, twined them with white roses and pink ribbons. She made bouquets of waxy tulips hidden in forests of fern. Posies of white violets were cunningly set into mossy containers, and she dug out a couple strings of fairy lights and all the pink candles she had in stock. At six, she loaded everything in her car and drove to the Grand Hotel.

She piled all the greenery in the living room and stepped back. There was a cozy fire in the fireplace—perfect. She started with the table, putting the violet posies behind the plates. Then she took some ivy and twined it around the candelabra in the middle of the table. To that, she added white rose buds. It matched the swath of ivy and white roses she tied to the mantle over the fireplace. Then she put the biggest bouquet, made of white lilac, pink roses, larkspur, tulips and lots of fern, on the table in front of the sofa, where the cocktail glasses were set up. She put the fairy lights in the ivy, and placed candles in flowered holders in strategic spots.

There was still one bouquet left: the pink tulips with the fern. She picked it up and looked for a place to put it. Finally, she set it on the mantle, after removing a framed picture of a rather stern looking man and woman. Seeing no place to put it, she shoved the picture under the couch.

She was done.

Just then the kitchen staff came up to deliver the dinner. "Can I help you?" Darla asked.

"Sure, grab this," said one, as the other waiter picked up a quiche.

Darla took a bowl of salad and opened the door to the small, efficiency kitchen Jordan had in his suite. She took off her coat and lay her purse on the counter as she helped put the food on the counters and in the oven. It looked like a real feast. There was salad and quiche, roast beef and a raspberry tart. The kitchen staff thanked her and left.

Darla had just gone back into the kitchen to fetch her purse, when the door opened.

In walked Jordan and Leslie.

Darla panicked. She did not want Jordan Severn to know that Darla Rooderville and Queenie Lovaday and Lilac Winters were all the same person. She definitely did not want Leslie to find out she was in his hotel suite. So she did what she thought was a good idea at the time. She ducked back into the kitchen and locked the door.

"Oh, this is beautiful!" cried Leslie. "Jordan, you are an angel. Mother and father will appreciate this."

Mother and father? Leslie's voice was strident, even when she wasn't shrieking at her. And was that what Leslie called her parents? Well, it was better than mummy and daddy, she supposed.

"When will they get here?" Jordan asked.

"I called my chauffeur on the cell phone. He picked them up at the airport and he'll be here in about twenty minutes," Leslie replied. There came the sound of ice clinking in a glass. "Make me a Shirley Temple, will you, darling?"

"About last night—" Jordan began, sounding a bit sheepish.

Darla strained to hear what he was going to say. What had they done last night? She hoped it wasn't much. No! She was going to stop craving Jordan. She pressed her ear closer to the door.

"Oh, it's all right. All men have that problem. I read about it in a woman's magazine. Besides, I really don't like taking a man's penis in my mouth. I hope you understand. I will be glad to help you if you feel you need to relieve your sexual tension, but I think it will be better if we wait until we're married. Then I'll be able to relax and enjoy myself." Leslie sounded convinced.

"You don't like, um, putting my penis in your mouth?" Jordan sounded less sure of himself.

Behind the kitchen door, Darla put both hands on her cheeks. How on earth had she gotten into this situation? And all that talk about penises. It was going to make her horny in no time. Especially since Jordan's penis was the subject of the conversation. She wondered what problem Leslie was referring to. Something she'd read about in a woman's magazine? Nothing serious, she hoped. Nah—she'd already seen and felt Jordan's cock hard and erect. It must be something else. But what?

"No. I don't particularly like putting a penis in my mouth," Leslie said.

"But, but Leslie, sex is supposed to be pleasurable for both parties." Jordan sounded stunned. Darla could sympathize. What was wrong with Leslie?

Leslie obviously found it necessary to explain. "Sex, if you think about it carefully, is an extremely degrading experience for a woman. She has to lie there while a . . . an enormous object is forced into her body."

Darla's knees buckled. "That sounds fine to me," she whispered. "Something hard and enormous. Oh, my." She was sitting on the floor, she realized, with her skirt hiked up around her waist and her hand between her legs. "Not again," she moaned.

Jordan laughed uncertainly. "Enormous? I don't consider my penis to be enormous."

"I do," sighed Darla. She pressed her hand against her clit then snatched it away. She was supposed to be trying to get over Jordan. She was going to control herself from now on and not get herself into any more debacles involving Jordan and Leslie. Right now, she should be planning her escape.

Leslie sniffed. "Maybe. At any rate, I just want you to know that I am open-minded and I will make every attempt to enjoy myself, but don't expect me to give you a blowjob unless it's once a year on your birthday."

"I'll drink to that," said Jordan. He didn't sound enthusiastic.

"Lighten up! Sex isn't everything."

"I happen to think it's an important part of a marriage," said Jordan. In the kitchen, Darla heaved a huge sigh. Poor Jordan sounded dismal. "I think it's important too," she whispered at the door. "Maybe Leslie isn't the right woman for you after all." This thought raised her spirits considerably.

"I thought we had this conversation already. You said that you were going to change." Leslie's voice climbed, raising gooseflesh on Darla's arms.

"I know, I know. But I'm starting to have second thoughts. I don't know, Leslie. I'd like to discuss this."

"I don't particularly want to discuss sex, especially with my parents around."

"They aren't even here yet!" Jordan was now starting to sound exasperated.

"Spoken like a true sexist male," said Leslie. Darla grinned. Evidently Leslie didn't know what to do with Jordan.

Jordan coughed. "Look, maybe we're rushing into things. We've only known each other a month and . . ."

"I don't want to talk about sex. End of conversation. Where is the food?" asked Leslie.

"In the kitchen," Jordan said.

Darla gasped in panic. Had he just said, "kitchen"?

"I'll just go check on it." Leslie tried the door handle. "It's locked."

"Impossible." Jordan tried it too. "You're right. Stay here, I'll go through the bedroom and unlock it."

"Good idea. I'll wait here in case my parents show up."

Darla looked around. Other door? Too late, she saw what she'd taken to be a broom closet door opening. She scrambled to her feet and looked for a place to hide. There was no place. She backed against the counter and braced herself.

Jordan opened the door, and stood, transfixed.

"Shhh." Darla held her finger to her lips. "Don't say anything," she whispered.

Jordan opened his mouth, doubtless to scream, thought Darla, but at that moment, there came the sound of the front door opening.

"Mother, father! Welcome! How was your flight? Come in! Mr. and Mrs. Severn, it's delightful to see you again," Leslie brayed.

Jordan put his hands on the counter to steady himself. "What are you doing here?" he asked in a soft voice.

"I was hired to do the flowers," whispered Darla. "Flower decorations."

"You do flowers too?" He rubbed his face. "If Leslie sees you, she will . . ." He stopped and looked grim. "She won't see you. You will not leave this room until the dinner is finished and everyone is gone. Is that clear?" His eyes narrowed and his voice was so stern and . . . masterful.

Darla's pussy reacted to Jordan's firm voice with a terrific jolt. Blazing heat shot through her cunt and flooded it with a heady rush of liquid. In a second, her underwear was sopping wet. Her nipples stood up at attention, poking at her shirt, and she swallowed with difficulty. She was in a predicament though, and she owed it to Jordan to try to make things go as smoothly as possible. After all, Leslie's father was his boss from what she'd understood. If she screwed this up, he would hate her forever.

"Yes," whispered Darla. He hadn't snatched up the carving knife and stabbed her. She tried to smile. It didn't work. Instead, a tear popped out of her eye and slid down her cheek.

Jordan looked stunned. "No, no, don't cry. I'm sorry. It's all right." He stepped towards her then stopped, a strange look on his face.

"What's the matter?"

"I don't know." He gave a little laugh. "I guess I can tell you. We've gone through enough already. It's just that when I see you, I get hard."

"Oh." Darla felt her cheeks burn.

"So we better avoid each other," continued Jordan. "I don't want to hurt your feelings, or compromise your, er, reputation."

Someone pounded on the door. "Jordan, is everything all right?"

"Yes, Leslie. I'm . . . just putting the . . . quiche in the oven," said Jordan, as Darla mimed what to say.

"Well, hurry. My parents are here." Leslie's voice dropped to a loud whisper. "What did you do with their picture?"

"I put it on the mantle," said Jordan in a sotto voice.

"It's not there," she hissed back.

"It has to be there."

"It isn't there. Where did you put it?" She sounded pissed.

"I'll be there in a second, and I'll look for it," said Jordan. He turned to Darla and he whispered to her, "Stay here. Do not unlock this door. I will say it is jammed. Do not go into my bedroom, there is no door to the living room and they will see you. Do you understand?"

"Yes."

"If, by some terrible mistake, Leslie should come in here, you will hide."

"Where?"

"Anywhere." For the first time he looked angry. "Anywhere at all." And before she could tell him where she put the picture, he swung around and left.

The wait was endless. First there were exclamations about Leslie's black eye.

"My baby! What happened to you!" cried her mother.

"Jordan can tell you," Leslie said in an icy voice.

"You'll never believe it," said Jordan, in what sounded like a forced attempt to laugh. "My friend Lars organized a party and he didn't know about Leslie, of course. He hired a girl to jump out of a cake."

"A stripper?" Leslie's mother sounded horrified.

"She punched me in the eye," Leslie whined.

"I need a drink," said her mother.

They had cocktails, and then there were champagne toasts to Jordan and Leslie.

Someone found the picture Darla had shoved beneath the sofa, and there was a dispute between Leslie and Jordan as to how it got there.

Then the dinner began.

Jordan rushed into the kitchen and grabbed the quiche. "Listen, while you're here, could you start the next course?" he whispered.

"Of course," Darla said. "It's no problem at all."

"Thanks. Listen, I'm sorry if I yelled at you earlier. I'm in sort of a bind here." He looked ruefully at the quiche. "I thought Leslie was perfect for me, but as usual, I've made a mess of things."

"You're doing fine," said Darla, feeling her heart warming to him. She'd never met a man before who would admit he'd made a mess of things.

He paused before leaving, and when Darla caught him looking at her, she thought she saw his eyes sparkle. It was just wishful thinking, she decided, as she made the salad dressing.

There was the quiche to start, and while they ate, Darla tossed the salad, put the roast filet of beef in the oven, then took the raspberry tart out of the freezer to thaw. Jordan ran in and out of the kitchen, and Darla cleaned up as quietly as possible.

Whenever he came in he'd say, "Is everything all right?" and he'd smile at her. He made her feel so . . . so something she'd never felt before. It was impossible to describe how she felt. It was as if her insides had suddenly turned into chocolate toffee, or something equally as wonderful. All the Valentine candy in the world wasn't sweeter than Jordan's smile.

"Oh Jordan, you are such a wonder in the kitchen," gushed the woman whom Darla had figured to be Leslie's mother. They had the same shrill voice.

Jordan's mother said, "Being away from home has certainly sharpened some skills. Tell me, Jordan, why didn't you ever serve dinner at home?"

"I can help," Leslie said. "Here, let me carry the plates to the kitchen. Did everyone have enough roast beef? I'll get that." Darla shrank against the wall, searching for a hiding place.

"No! Sit down! I mean, no, Leslie. Here, just sit and relax. I'll do everything," Jordan insisted. Darla's heartbeat returned to almost normal. Almost, because every time she heard Jordan's voice, it started pounding again. Honestly. What a time to fall in love!

"Oh Leslie, you certainly found a pearl," cried her mother, bringing Darla back to reality.

For the time being, Jordan was Leslie's, not hers. She sighed.

"I'll say," said Jordan's mother, a question in her voice. "I had no idea you were so proficient," she added.

Jordan brought the dinner plates in, but there was no more room to put everything, so Darla filled the sink with dish soap and put the dishes in to soak. "What's next?" he asked.

"Dessert. Here are the plates. I'll start warming the tart. It will be about ten minutes, so everyone can relax."

"Thanks," said Jordan. He reached for a napkin and their hands collided. He didn't pull away. For a second, Darla even thought he might reach over and touch her cheek, but he straightened and cleared his throat.

"Sorry," he said. His cheeks were red.

Darla shrugged. "No problem." She wished he would leave. Not only because his presence nearly made her forget her vow and every time she saw him her cunt throbbed, but because now she had to pee so badly she thought she would explode.

She'd eaten in the kitchen, helping herself to salad and quiche, but no beef; she was a vegetarian. She drank a few glasses of wine, after uncorking the bottles for Jordan. She'd drunk a whole bottle of Perrier water. She really had to pee. "Go on, I'll be fine here."

Jordan nodded, took a deep breath, and left.

Darla peered through the forbidden door leading to Jordan's bedroom. The bathroom was on the other side of the bedroom. To get to it, she would have to pass in front of the arched doorway leading to the dining room. She would be in full view of everyone. That was out of the question.

What to do?

She eyed the sink. It was full of soapy water and dishes. Well, desperate times called for desperate measures. She knew urine was sterile, so she didn't feel bad about peeing in the sink. She'd wash it out afterwards.

She took the dishes and carefully stacked them on the counter. With her elbow, she knocked the dish soap on the floor. She picked it up, but not before half of it had poured out.

Oh no! The noise! "Be quiet," she hissed to herself.

Hopping, her legs crossed, she drained the sink. When she was done, there was soapy water everywhere. She made sure there was nothing more in the sink, and then she took off her skirt, her shoes, her stockings and her underwear and put them on a chair in the corner. There was not much space in the kitchen. She climbed up on the sink and sat.

She had to pee. She knew she had to pee. So why couldn't she pee? It was like one of those awful dreams, where you're in front of a crowd of people and you find yourself sitting on a toilet. Nothing happened.

Darla sighed and closed her eyes. She pictured herself in a real bathroom, sitting on a real toilet, with the door closed and no one around for miles. There, that helped. In a minute, she started to pee. Oh, that felt so much better. She ran some warm water to rinse the sink, and to rinse herself.

The warm water felt nice. There was a little hose for rinsing the dishes. She could turn the spray right on her clit. She was starting to enjoy this.

She made herself more comfortable, and splashed a little more water over her pussy. But she still ached for Jordan. She wished he'd straighten everything out and break up with Leslie, and then she could go about making him hers, for she'd decided that Jordan was the man of her dreams, even if he didn't realize it yet.

Her hand somehow found its way to her cunt, and before she knew it, she was stroking herself, leaning back on the sink, her legs dangling. The water on her clit was like a clever finger. She could turn the water down and make it soft, or spray harder, and then really get some action.

Her pussy clenched, and she moaned softly as she heard Jordan's voice. His sexy, sexy voice. She felt her face flush. Here she was, half naked, just a few yards away from him. If he came in he'd see her, her legs wide open, her fingers dipping into her pussy as she stroked herself. Her labia were swelling, pressing together.

She was just getting into the rhythm, slipping a finger into her cunt and wiggling it a bit, when suddenly a sound made her frown.

The sound was Leslie's voice saying, "Who on earth is in the kitchen, Jordan?"

Darla froze. Shivers ran up her spine as she realized what she was doing. This was not good. She was not acting in a responsible manner. Her oversexed body was once again ruling her mind. How could she be so lacking in judgment? She was a grown woman, after all, with a good business. Last she'd looked, she'd had a head on her shoulders. She would just have to learn to use it, that's all.

Jordan started to stammer, when his mother said, "Jordan has always been helpless in the kitchen. I bet he got one of the hotel staff to help him and he was afraid to admit it."

"That's right," said Jordan. "Ah mom, I can't fool you, can I?"

"Well, that's settled," said Leslie. "Honestly. You silly boy. Why don't you tell the waiter to bring out the coffee?"

"Uh, I'll go tell, er, the waiter," said Jordan.

Darla panicked. She leaped off the sink, hit the soapy water on the floor, and crashed into Jordan just as he entered the kitchen. His feet knocked clear out from under him, he fell, this time on top of Darla.

They tried to untangle themselves, but the soap was too slippery and they ended up skidding across the floor. Darla hooked her legs around Jordan's thigh to keep from hitting the wall.

"Are you okay?" asked Jordan, getting up on his elbows and peering down at her.

Darla looked up at him. "I think I broke my back. I can't move my arms or legs."

"Oh my God!" Jordan said.

"Shhh. I'm sorry. I'm just joking." Darla wriggled. "See? I'm fine. You just knocked the breath out of me, that's all."

"You scared me."

"I said I was sorry."

Her mouth was next to his. It was too irresistible. She kissed him lightly on his lips. He answered by pressing his lips firmly on hers, and giving her a deep, sexy kiss. His lips roamed over hers, and a deep purr grew in her throat. Jordan nibbled gently on her lower lip, and then his tongue stole a taste of her mouth. She ran her tongue over the inside of his lip, then fastened her teeth on it, tugging a bit. The kiss degenerated into a mini-wrestling match of tongues. She moaned softly, her nipples tingling and standing up at attention.

"That was nice," she breathed, when they came up for air.

Jordan didn't answer. He put his forehead on her shoulder and gave a little moan.

"Are you all right?" Darla was worried. She wriggled again, and this time she felt what the problem was. It was an enormous problem. She closed her eyes, overcome by emotion. Enormous was how she liked them. Her legs, wrapped around his muscular thighs, tightened.

"Are you all right in there, Jordan?" His mother's voice sounded worried.

"I'm fine. I'm helping the waiter," he croaked.

"Make coffee," whispered Darla. "I'm helping the waiter make coffee and we're preparing the raspberry tart."

"We're getting tart and making raspberry coffee," Jordan cried. He put his forehead on Darla's shoulder. "This is not right."

"It feels all right," said Darla.

"I can't serve coffee like this." He glared at her, but it lacked conviction. "You're naked from the waist down. What were you doing?"

Darla hoped her grin didn't look too stupid. "I was peeing in the sink."

Jordan blinked. "In the sink?"

"There is no toilet in the kitchen, and I didn't think you wanted me to show myself to anyone."

"Except me," said Jordan. He groaned again. "I hope you don't mind, but I think I'm about to . . . " He broke off and his hips gave a little thrust. "I can't help it," he gasped.

"Wait!" Darla ordered. She reached down and unbuckled his belt. "The least you can do is put me out of my misery at the same time," she gasped.

"What are you talking about?" he whispered, as her hand found his fly and hastily unbuttoned it.

"If I don't get your cock into my pussy in five seconds flat, I will start to scream," she said. She took his hand and slipped it between her legs, pressing his fingers into her slick, swollen pussy. "See?"

Jordan's eyebrows lifted. "Wow." He swallowed hard. "Well, might as well be hung for a sheep as for a lamb."

"No, this is an ox," said Darla, opening his fly and grasping his penis in her hands. "Come on, put it right in here."

"Are you on the Pill?" he asked.

"Yes," Darla said. "Promise, cross my heart. I've never had anything contagious; I haven't slept with anyone in a year. Oh Jordan. Please, please. Or I will . . . Oh my! Yes!" she gasped.

He pushed up onto his elbow and slid the tip of his penis into her cunt. With his hand, he guided himself into her. Once his cock touched her labia, Darla felt her whole cunt blossom. She was tight, and Jordan was big, but she raised her hips into the air, pulling him into her using both ends of his unbuckled belt.

Slowly, he sheathed himself inside her. Inch by inch he slid into her pussy. It was too good. It was incredibly good. It was chocolate fudge toffee times ten-thousand. Her legs trembled in delight and she gave a long, shivery moan. He filled her, he filled her completely. She felt her cunt throbbing, and she knew she was about to come. "It's been too long," she whispered, and she arched her back and gave in to the sensations swirling through her. "I'm coming," she gasped. "Come with me!"

He didn't need any encouragement. Bracing himself on his elbows, he thrust into her, sliding in and out the whole length of his cock. The feel of it leaving her body then entering again was overwhelming. Every part of her body was glowing. Her cunt was contracting around him, the ring of muscle clasping Jordan's cock in a fervent handshake.

Jordan thrust once, twice, three times, while her body writhed beneath his. Then his control shattered and he ground his hips into hers, pressing his face into the crook of her neck while he ejaculated wildly inside her.

And that's when Leslie entered the picture and started to scream.

Of course, that brought everyone running. They stopped in the doorway and stared.

Darla stared back. She was half naked, half squashed and totally embarrassed.

"What is going on?" trumpeted a man.

"Who is that?" screeched a woman, who looked just like Leslie. Right down to the navy blue suit she wore.

"What are they doing?" cried another man.

"If he doesn't know what we're doing, he must be Leslie's father," whispered Darla, and she started to giggle.

"Good heavens," said Jordan's mother, leaning over to get a good look. "Is that the new uniform for the waiters at the hotel?"

"You beast! You're disgusting. I wouldn't be caught dead with you!" Leslie screamed.

"Young man, you're fired!" bellowed Leslie's father.

"I don't think so." It was Jordan's father; he looked more than a bit amused, thought Darla with some confusion.

"What do you mean?" Leslie screeched. "Of course he's fired! It's my father's hotel."

"It was. I bought it from him last week. Signed the final papers last night. Didn't I Mr. Tarryalot?" Jordan's father shrugged. "It was going to be my wedding present to my son."

"God, I'm so glad I broke up with you. I would rather die than live here in these boonies," cried Leslie.

"I'm going to have a migraine," announced Leslie's mother. "If I don't get out of this place, I'm going to have a migraine."

"For heaven's sake—get out of here then," cried Jordan's mother.

The three Tarryalots stormed out of the kitchen and out of the suite, slamming the door behind them.

Darla lay perfectly still. Perhaps no one would really notice her, and she would be able to sneak out. Jordan gallantly kept her covered with his body, and he looked down at her with a very embarrassed grin. "Sorry," he whispered.

"No, I'm not," Darla answered, although she knew he'd been apologizing.

He grinned.

"Please," said Darla and Jordan at the same time, "we can explain everything."

"This, I have to hear," said Jordan's mother. "Why don't we let this young lady get dressed? Jordan, no, don't move. Wait until we leave. We'll be waiting for you in the living room."

When the door shut, Jordan heaved himself onto his elbows and looked down at Darla. "You realize you have just ruined my life," he said, his eyes dancing with barely suppressed mirth.

"It depends which way you look at it," she answered. "I heard what Leslie said about sex. I might have just saved your life."

He looked abashed. "I was having second and third thoughts, to tell you the truth."

She looked at him, and then noticed his clothes. "You're all wet. Let me help you with those pants."

"What?"

She sat up and took his pants off the rest of the way, sliding them off his long, muscular legs and tossing them to the corner of the kitchen. "Take off your shoes."

He did. She took his foot and examined it. "Greek toes. The second toe is longer than your big toe," she explained, catching his puzzled look. "You have very sexy feet." She loved beautiful hands and feet. Jordan's feet were narrow with the tendons clearly marked. His hands were strong and capable looking, with long fingers.

"Thank you. I can say the same for yours," he said, leering at her bare feet. Then, without waiting for her to ask, took off his shirt and his tie.

Darla nodded in approval. "That's right." She took her sopping wet sweater off and flung it on the growing pile of clothes. "Your turn."

He slid out of his boxer shorts.

"Oh my," whispered Darla. "It's hard again." She reached over and put her hand on the most magnificent cock she'd ever dreamed of. "It's bigger and better than Eden," she cried.

He unhooked her bra and took it off. Then he took her breasts, one in each hand, and gently squeezed. "I've been dreaming of this since I met you," he said.

"Oh, that reminds me." She stood up, carefully because of the slick floor, and sang in her best, Marilyn Monroe imitation, "Here's a gift for you on your birthday, here's a present for you. I hope you have a happy birthday, and may all your wishes come true." She wiggled a bit, making her tits bounce. Then she did an impromptu belly dance. It was getting hard to move, because the floor was soapy, and because she was so aroused that her labia were swollen twice their normal size. She clenched her thighs together.

"Come here," he said, pointing to the floor.

"Yes master," Darla said, demurely. She knelt before him. "What do you desire?" She shivered in anticipation.

"Anything you want to do is fine by me," said Jordan. His voice was a bit raw, she noticed. He kneeled and drew his fingers around her silky pubic hair. "It's a heart," he said.

"Do you like it?"

"It suits you," he said, his fingers delving into her pussy and gently parting her labia. He hesitated, then inserted one finger into her vagina and penetrated, slowly, in and out.

She reached down and stroked his cock again. It was perfect. With a happy sigh, she leaned over and slid it into her mouth. Her tongue working, she sucked as much cock as she could into her mouth. Humming, she tickled his thighs while she gently bobbed her head up and down. His cock was luscious, like the rest of him.

Jordan was perfect, absolutely perfect, and Darla was so happy she thought her heart would burst.

"You'd better stop," he whispered, his hand still cupping her pussy, his finger still teasing inside her cunt, setting her on fire.

She raised her head and grinned. "Oh?" His cock was like a rock in her hand. She squeezed it gently. It was so hard! A rush of heat flooded her belly. Her cunt contracted on his finger. "I think you better lie down."

"I think so too," he agreed. He withdrew his hand and lay down on the floor.

"Well, how about this?" Darla lay next to him and rubbed herself against him. The floor was slippery and so were their bodies. Jordan's hard cock pressed into her thigh. Actually, Jordan was hard all over, thought Darla. His shoulders were broad, his arms muscular, his chest was hard, his belly was flat with tight abs, and he had a strip of dark hair snaking up from his pubis to his belly button. She followed it backwards with her hand, twining her fingers in his curly pubic hair.

When he grabbed her, his hands slipped. He tried to grasp her breasts, but they were slippery as well. He put both hands on her ass and squeezed. "You have a magnificent ass," he murmured.

Darla took his cock, and slipped it into her hot and juicy cunt. He took her breasts and gently pinched her nipples, while she slid against him and then rolled over and straddled him. Now she could look down as she rocked back and forth. His cock was so big it filled her and stretched her to the limit. It felt like heaven. He kept his hands on her breasts, kneading and stroking, and pinching her nipples. Leaning forward, she spread her knees as far apart as she could and speared herself on him, using the slippery floor to her advantage as she rose and fell on his cock. Her breath came in gasps. Throwing her head back, she cried, "Yes! Yes! Yes!"

"Miss Lilac?" gasped Jordan. "That was you?"

"Hush," Darla said. She turned around, still impaled on his cock, so that she was facing backwards. Then she rose on her knees, sliding up and down his cock. She leaned forward a bit. "Do you really like my butt?" she asked, hooking her chin over her shoulder to stare at him.

He licked his lips. "It's incredible," he said.

"You should see what it can do," Darla purred.

"Will you show me?"

"Watch." She slid off his cock, and then sat on the soapy floor. When she got up, her butt was covered in suds. "Nice and slippery," she said.

Jordan laid there, his cock sticking straight into the air. His chest was rising and falling quickly. Darla was practically purring with delight. She straddled him once more, this time facing him, and carefully put his cock into her anus. Slowly, wriggling around in a little circle with her hips, she thrust down upon him. As she did so, she widened her knees, so that her pussy was open like a flower before him.

"Take me with your hands," she ordered.

He groaned, arching his back as she started to rise and fall, contracting the muscles in her buttocks around his cock. His hands reached for her and found her, trembling, he inserted one, then another finger. He thrust in time to her movements.

Darla moved faster, sliding her hips forward, forcing his fingers deeper into her slick cunt. She reached down and rubbed her clit at the same time. Her whole body was starting to pulse.

Jordan suddenly stiffened, arched his back and dug his fingers deep into her cunt. "I'm coming," he yelled, and held her hips while his cock spurted into her ass.

Darla thought her head was going to explode. Instead, it was her cunt. It went off in a starburst of earth-shattering contractions around his hand that made her scream, "Jordan! Jordan! Oh, yes!"

Afterwards, she collapsed onto his chest, her heart pounding, her head spinning, and her whole body glowing.

"Do you think we can get up now?" asked Jordan.

"Only if it's to crawl as far as your bed," answered Darla.

"Sounds good to me."

Darla got to her knees and crawled across the kitchen floor. It was slippery and she was tingling all over. "Do you feel as good as I do?" she asked Jordan.

"Better," he assured her, with a kiss.

Darla made it to the bedroom, still on her knees. Then she crawled onto the bed and collapsed. "Jordan," she said.

"Yes?"

"Kiss me, please." She opened her arms and he cuddled into them, kissing her gently on the lips.

He pulled back and pushed a lock of hair out of her eyes. "Is it possible to fall in love at first sight?" he asked her.

Darla hesitated. "I don't know," she admitted. "If it is, then I guess that's what happened to me." She felt her cheeks burning.

"What is it?"

"I'm not usually so fast," she said in a low voice.

Jordan chuckled. "I think I fell in love with you the second you jumped out of the cake."

Darla stifled a giggle. "That's when I hit Leslie."

"That's not very nice," said Jordan. He grinned. "I fell in love with you before you hit Leslie."

"That was fast," said Darla. She pulled him to her and kissed him again.

They stopped, and looked towards the living room.

"Your parents are still here," whispered Darla. "Do you think I can dig a hole and hide?"

"Can you dig one big enough for both of us?" said Jordan.

"At least they put the music on," said Darla. "I'll just get under these covers. You go sort things out."

"Um, I need to know your name," said Jordan.

Darla blinked. "Why?"

"Because, I need to tell them whom I'm going to marry," said Jordan, putting his arms around her. "I've discovered the girl of my dreams in a collapsible cake, and I can't just say Miss Lilac. Hey—why are you crying?"

"Because, no one has ever asked me to marry them before."

"I hope that means yes," said Jordan. He kissed her. "I really hope that means yes. Because I can't stand thinking of not being able to run into my nutty woman anymore. I'm hoping to run into her at least once a day."

"At least?" Darla dried her eyes and drew a deep breath. "How wonderful."

"Are you happy?" he asked, kissing her again.

"Why don't you come under these covers and see?" she said. Her voice wavered, and she thought maybe she would cry again. She had never, ever been so happy in her life. The man of her dreams had just proposed to her. It was as if she really had a fairy godmother. She felt like Cinderella. No, she felt better than Cinderella.

"In a minute. I'll just go see my parents and I'll be right back. They won't be mad, don't worry. I know them." He sounded rueful. "My mom never liked Leslie," he added in a whisper.

"Couldn't stand her." Jordan's mother's voice rose over the music.

"Hush, Georgette," said her husband.

"See?" said Jordan.

"You don't have to get out of bed," said his father. He stood up and said, "Come on Georgette, let's leave Jordan and . . ."

"Darla," whispered Darla.

"Darla. I'm marrying Darla," said Jordan. "She did the flower arrangements."

"We're pleased to meet you, Darla. We'll see you at breakfast tomorrow. Know any good places to go?" his father asked.

"Doyle's Donuts. We'll be there at ten," said Darla.

The door closed and Darla sat up in bed. "You don't have to marry me," she said, touching him lightly on the chin.

"Yes, I do," Jordan answered, taking her finger and kissing it. "I fell in love with you."

"But Jordan, I don't want to rush into anything. Look what happened with you and Leslie. You didn't know her well enough."

"What would you like to do?" Jordan asked, leaning back in bed and cuddling her next to him.

"I want to live together for six months, while we plan our wedding. And if we can live through that, we can live through anything."

Jordan thought about that for a minute, then kissed her lips. "Deal. Now, can we go take a bath together?"

Darla grinned wickedly. "With lots of bubbles?"

"Slippery bubbles?" Jordan swallowed and closed his eyes.

"Slippery, bubbly bubbles." Darla sighed happily. "I'm engaged to the man I love," she whispered, trailing a line of kisses over his collarbone.

"And I am engaged to the woman I love—Miss Lilac."

Darla choked back a laugh. "No, you're not engaged to Miss Lilac. She's a hundred and four."

"All right, so you're not Miss Lilac, and you're not Queenie Lovaday. Who are you?"

"Darla Rooderville, local flowershop owner, nature lover, trail rider and madly in love with you."

Jordan kissed the tip of her nose. "Sounds perfect to me."

$\mathcal{S}ix$

Darla's Secret

"I'm NOT GOING to tell my parents right away about you being a jump out of a cake girl," said Jordan. "We'll wait a few weeks, all right?" Jordan cuddled next to her, then stiffened. "The note on the bouquet. It had Darla written on it!"

"It did?" Darla frowned. "It said Darla?"

"It did." He sounded stern.

"I don't know how that happened. I'm sorry. I was pretty tired when I wrote the note. What can I say?"

"How about, happy Valentine's Day?" said Jordan.

"Sounds about right to me." She kissed him and then nibbled on his lip. "Can you do something for me?"

"What?"

"Go wash off. Then come back and I'll show you a game."

"What about the bath?"

"It will have to wait."

"All right." He looked mystified, but he did as she'd asked. When he came back, Darla said, "Put you hand right—yes. That's it. Right between my legs. Now rub harder. And while you're doing that, I'm going to be on the phone."

"You're going to be what?"

"I'm going to call my best friend in the whole world, Wendy, and tell her all about my weekend. And you are going to leave your hand there. In fact, you're going to do everything in your power to make me come again while I'm on the phone."

Jordan looked shocked. "What?"

"I have something to tell you. I'm not a jump out of the cake girl. I was taking over for my best friend when I met you. It was the first time I'd ever tried jumping out of a cake."

"You were just a stand-in jump out of the cake girl?"

"Wendy went to a showgirl convention in Miami. She's the jump out of a cake girl."

"And she's your best friend?"

"Exactly. We're also the same height, the same weight, and have almost the same color hair. When we met each other in kindergarten, we knew it was fate. We were like sisters." She held up her hand and crossed her fingers. "We were always this close."

"Oh yeah? And how do I tell you apart?" he asked with a mischievous grin.

Darla grinned. "I like it up my ass," she said. "And Wendy gives the best blow-jobs north of Buenos Aires."

There was a large pause. "You're sure about that?" Jordan whispered.

"Yeah. Someone said there was a gal in Patagonia who held the world record. Wendy said she'd settle for second place."

"Christ. I'm getting hard again."

"Good, because her phone is ringing. Hello? Wendy? How was the convention?"

Darla winked at Jordan and put on the loudspeaker. "Darla? Is that you? It's late!"

"What do you mean, it's late?"

"I've been waiting for your call for an hour."

"I've been busy."

Wendy gasped. "Did you find a boyfriend?"

"Better! I'm engaged! And guess what—it's Jordan Severn," Darla crowed. She took Jordan's hand and rubbed it on her cunt. "Harder, and with two fingers," she whispered.

There was a silence at the end of the wire. "I heard that," said Wendy. She paused. "Is he doing it now?"

"Yes." Darla lay back and raised her hips. "He is. And he has the most incredible cock in the world."

"Lucky Darla," sighed Wendy. "Tell me the whole story! I'm all wet just thinking about it. What's he doing now?"

Darla grinned. "We share everything," she explained to Jordan. "Think you can get used to it?"

He slid his fingers back and forth. "Why don't you reach down and see?" he asked.

She did and gasped. "Oh Lord, Wendy. He's good for number three."

"How is it, tell me!" she cried.

"It's long and thick, with a head the size of a plum. You just want to suck it all night."

"That's what I'm best at," agreed Wendy.

"He's excited now. Wait a sec, I'm going to sit on him."

"Put the phone near so I can hear it!" begged Wendy.

"What are you doing?"

"Actually, I'm lying on my stomach."

"Really?"

"And someone is kneeling over me."

"Who?" Darla asked. She drew her breath in with a hiss as Jordan parted her labia and twirled a finger into her cunt.

"Remember Carlos? The man I told you about last year?"

"The one you met the last convention, but you lost his phone number?"

"Well, he lost mine too, and when we met, we knew that this time we had to make it real."

"And?" Darla poised herself over Jordan's cock, and then slowly eased onto it. "I'm being stabbed by an enormous cock, right into the center of my swollen pussy. Oh lord, Wendy, it feels so good. You should see Jordan. He is so stiff it's unbelievable. I feel like I'm sitting on a wooden post."

"Well, Carlos is in my cunt, darling Darla. He's not moving, because he's listening to your sexy voice, but I can feel him spurting a little. I think he's about to lose control. My husband is . . ."

"Your what?" Darla gave a shout and shoved herself down to the hilt of Jordan's cock.

"Husband. We're married. Civil ceremony in Miami. We'll do it right in the spring up north. You'll do the flowers, of course. Hold on, he's thrusting like mad. Whoa, easy tiger! If you want to play rough, you'll have to go see my friend Darla."

Darla gave a strangled scream. "Oh, yes. Play rough. Did you hear her Jordan? Show me what you can do."

"She loves a good spanking," said Wendy. "Oh, excuse me, I don't think I'll be able to talk for a while. Yes, Yes, Oh yes, Carlos! Harder!"

Jordan needed no encouragement. He sat up, and then slid out of Darla's cunt. He turned her over on his lap and gave her a little slap.

"No, make it sting," she begged. She loved having her ass sticking up in the air and feeling his erection pressing against her stomach.

"I don't want to hurt you," he said.

"Then don't, just give me a nice little spanking." She writhed and lifted her butt higher into the air. "Make sure Wendy can hear."

"All right." He slapped her until her cheeks were rosy and her cunt was dripping onto his thighs. Then he sat her on his lap and penetrated her cunt with his cock, bouncing her as she begged him to go harder and faster.

"Wendy!" she cried, "I'm coming!"

She screamed into the phone, and then dropped it on the bed as she raised her butt and grasped Jordan's shoulders, pulling him into her all the way; until she couldn't begin to tell where he began and she left off. Her cunt pulsed and contracted around his cock. "So good!" she screamed.

Jordan picked up the phone. "Are you still there?" he asked.

"Of course."

"Well, now I'm going to pull out of Darla's cunt."

"Hey, give me that phone," said Darla. "This is our game."

"It's mine too now," said Jordan. He winked at her, and she felt a stab of pure delight. Stan had been horrified and she'd had to keep their game secret. "Tell her what you're doing," she said.

"Hi Wendy, this is Jordan."

"Hi! You can thank me for Darla. I convinced her to jump out of the cake for your birthday."

"I'll have to find a way to show my gratitude," said Jordan.

"Well, Carlos and I will talk about it and see what we can come up with. So, what are you doing to Darla's hot little body right now?"

Jordan raised his eyebrows and Darla nodded. "I'm easing out of her hot, tight cunt. She just about squeezed me dry with her last orgasm, but I still have a bit left. I'm still hard and horny, to tell you the truth."

"Oh baby, if only I was there to put my lips around it and make it better. I'd suck you up and down and sideways."

"I'm sure you would. But now I have Darla on her hands and knees here, and she's rubbing her ass against my cock. What should I do?"

"If I were you, I'd grab her around the waist with both hands and I'd shove my cock as deep down as it will go."

"Sounds like a good idea," said Jordan. He handed the phone back to Darla. "Talk to your best friend—if you can," he said, arching his back and pulling Darla towards him by the waist at the same time. He slid into her slowly, easing past the tight ring of muscle, and then, making sure he was properly lubricated with her juices, he started to thrust.

"Oh, Wendy," gasped Darla. "This is the most incredible experience. Hey! Is that your husband spanking your butt?"

"He's just doing it to turn you on, you naughty girl."

Darla gasped. "It worked, I'm drenched. And Jordan is so big he can hardly move in my butt. He's going slowly right now, but I want some more action and at least three fingers in my cunt. Oh yes! Go on, harder!"

"Ouch, Carlos!" Wendy giggled. "He spanked my butt too hard. Hold on, I'm going to make him apologize."

"How?"

"He's got to suck my breasts."

"Oh, that's another thing," groaned Darla, as Jordan thrust into her.

"What?" he gasped. He was short of breath. Darla could tell he was fighting for control. "What thing is that?"

"Wendy has bigger breasts than I do, and she loves to have her nipples stroked and sucked."

"And you?"

"I prefer tickling my clit. Will you please, no, leave your fingers where they are, use your thumb, oh yes! Oh, I am so wet."

"I bet you are," said Wendy, purring over the phone. "Carlos has a mouthful of nipple, or else he'd say hello. I like having a finger on my clit too, but right now, I'm pushing Carlos's head south. Did you hear that pop? It was my nipple coming out of his sweet mouth. Go south young man, and pleasure your mistress-wife with your hot tongue."

Jordan grabbed Darla's breasts with his free hand, and bending over her neck, said, "I am about to explode. Will you please hang up?"

"Why?"

"I don't want your friend to hear me scream. At least not until we've been properly introduced."

"Got to go, Wendy," said Darla, trying to keep her voice level. Actually, she felt like screaming too.

"Oh yes!" cried Wendy, "Carlos, your mouth is on fire! Goodbye Darla, see you in a few days!"

Darla tossed the phone back on the hook and leaned into Jordan. "Don't be afraid. Thrust baby, thrust! Shove hard!" she said.

He complied, crying out in a hoarse voice as his whole body convulsed. Darla stayed perfectly still, eyes closed, concentrating on the pulsing she felt as it spread to her cunt and she started a mad pulsing around Jordan's fingers.

"I can feel you coming," he cried, and shuddered once more, his cock twitching inside her ass.

Darla emptied herself on his hand. It felt as if she gushed as her cunt contracted and pulsed. She could hardly breathe, and the bed seemed to toss and turn as she arched her back and called Jordan's name.

They collapsed in a heap on the bed, and it was a while before Darla could get up and stagger as far as the bathroom, where she ran a hot bath. She added some bubbles.

"I am going to be so sore tomorrow," she said, as she leaned back and relaxed in the water.

"Move over," said Jordan, stepping in.

"Love these luxury hotels. Baths big enough for two."

"Or three or four." He leaned over and kissed her. "Do you share everything with your best friend?"

"We've never tried a ménage a trois or quatre, but that doesn't mean we never will. We're pretty highly sexed. I'm warning you right now. I get off on sex, and I expect my husband to get off on sex too. But I won't tolerate unfaithfulness, and I'll never be unfaithful," said Darla seriously. "I am a one man woman. When I marry, it will be for keeps. I want lots of children, and my husband is expected to share with the housework, chores and raising the family."

"I like families, I respect women, and I'm not the type to screw around," said Jordan. He grinned. "And I've been accused of being oversexed."

"Then you're just my type." Darla smiled. "I can't wait to introduce you to Wendy."

"I can't wait to meet her." Jordan raised his eyebrows. "Do you have phone sex often?"

"Whenever we can. Sometimes we just make it up." Darla shrugged. "We're pretty ordinary otherwise. We don't sleep around. As a matter of fact, you're only my third lover. My first one was my high school sweetheart, the second a disaster named Stan, and you're my number three."

"Lucky number three."

"*Licky* number three." She kissed his mouth and licked his lips.

"And Wendy?"

"Wendy is a little more experienced than I am. She thought she'd shock her parents by being gay for a year, and she announced it at dinner one night. Her mom said it was just a phase, and it was. She knew Wendy too well." Darla laughed. "My parents were horrified, but Wendy's mom talked to them and they calmed down enough to let me invite her over again."

"And did you ever, you know, with a girl?"

"Well, with Wendy. She wanted to show me what she did with her girlfriend. I told her I only liked it with her."

"What did she do to you?"

"Well, first she stroked my breasts, like this." Darla grinned impishly and drew circles around her nipples with a handful of bubbles. "Then she . . ."

"Shh. We had better change the subject."

Darla nodded and bit her lip. "I understand. I'm sorry I shocked you, but I'm one of those people who can't hide a thing. I'm oversexed, so is my best friend, and we sometimes go a little crazy. Jordan, if you don't want to marry me, it's no big deal. I know I can be a little overwhelming at times. It was nice of you to ask, but I won't hold you to it."

Jordan sank down in the bubbles and peered at her. His eyes were smoldering. "Did I say I was shocked?"

"Well, no," Darla admitted. "But I scared away my last boyfriend when I admitted everything. I decided I would always be up front about my sex life from then on."

"I've always had a problem. But I've never admitted it to anyone except my parents."

"Do you want to tell me about it?" Darla asked.

"If we're going to get married, I feel I have to," Jordan said, looking very serious.

Seven

Where Jordan Tells About His Enormous Problem

Jordan cleared his throat. "You have to see things from my point of view now. Ever since I was in high school, I've had sex on my mind. If I even thought about a girl, I got a hard-on. When I saw girls, it was even worse. I spent quite a bit of time running to the boy's room and masturbating.

"It wasn't anything too unusual. I knew a few other guys like myself—and my parents were more than understanding. When I told them about my problem, they made it clear that I wasn't a freak, but that I would have to learn to control myself. So I did. And everything would go great, until I started dating. As soon as a girl showed herself willing to sleep with me, I fell in love. But none of them could handle me." He stopped and blushed. "They just couldn't understand that I wanted to screw them morning, noon and night. After a month, they would break up with me."

"Oh Jordan!" Darla closed her eyes. Her body quivered. "Morning, noon and night?"

"Afraid so." Jordan looked depressed. "It is not a thing a man likes to admit, but I had my heart broken so much, I decided that the pain wasn't worth it. When I met Leslie, and she resisted me, I figured it was perfect. We would get married, and then she would turn me into the perfect husband, while I would show her the wonders of sex."

"And she would run screaming from the room." Darla grinned.

"That was a low blow."

"Aren't you glad I punched her in the eye?"

"It was a mistake." Jordan chuckled. "You didn't do it on purpose."

"Oh Jordan, I hope we'll be happy together." Darla slid over and put her arms around him, pulling herself onto his lap. Her eyes widened. "You have a hard-on!" she cried.

"It was that story about you and Wendy. I keep seeing the two of you lying in bed together with your hands on each other's breasts, and . . . well, you feel the result."

"You were made for me in heaven," said Darla.

"Then I guess that means no more broken hearts for me."

"I promise, cross my heart. If you want to screw me morning, noon and night, you will make me the happiest girl in the world."

Jordan caught her face in his hands and kissed her on the lips. "I am going to be so sore tomorrow," he said in a husky whisper. "But if you want to make me scream again, be my guest."

"Can I tell you about Wendy and me while I'm at it?" Darla asked, positioning herself right above his cock.

"Please," he gasped.

She slid her hips forward, sheathing herself in one, smooth movement on his cock. "We love to eat each other out. We slide our fingers into each other's cunts, and we lick our clits until they're stiff as little cocks. We suck on each other's nipples, and then we rub ourselves against each other," Darla whispered in his ear while she humped back and forth.

"Now tell me about me and you," said Jordan, his voice husky.

"When you look at me, I feel as if I'm a goddess. You make me feel as if I'm wonderful, and when you told me you loved me, it was as if all my dreams suddenly came true." Darla stopped. Leaning over, she kissed him. Inside her cunt, she felt his cock throbbing. She moved gently, making waves in the tub.

"Go on," Jordan whispered. He swallowed, and Darla saw the muscles work in his throat.

"When you touch me, my body turns to molten gold. It's as if I'm made of something rich and smooth. Your cock is the most incredible cock in the world. When it's inside me, like this, I want it to last forever. I can feel your heart beat inside my cunt. I can feel your . . ." her voice trailed off and she moved her hips faster.

A pulsing was growing in her belly. Her orgasm was making her whole body tingle, but it was sharpest deep in her cunt.

Jordan gave a strangled cry and thrust his cock into her as hard as he could. He grabbed her hips and held her tightly.

Soon she could feel him start to quiver, and when he let his head fall back and started to moan, she thought about all the ways they could make love together, for the rest of their lives, and she arched her back and let out a scream.

"Oh, Yes!"

The End
(Where Everyone Lives Happily Ever After)

ELLORA'S CAVE PRESENTS...

SIZZLING COLLECTIONS OF SENSUAL STORIES
FROM YOUR FAVORITE ELLORA'S CAVE WRITERS!

Some men just can't be tamed…but it sure is fun to try with these stories by Kimberly Dean, Summer Devon, and Michelle Pillow.

Unwrap these sexy stories by Jaid Black, Shiloh Walker, and Dominique Adair.

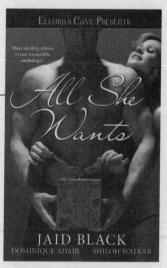

Available wherever books are sold or at www.simonsayslove.com.

Visit www.EllorasCave.com.

15671

POCKET BOOKS
A Division of Simon & Schuster
A CBS COMPANY